THOSE SWEET WORDS

A MISFIT INN NOVEL

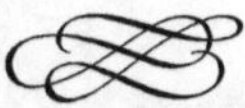

KAIT NOLAN

For C. No matter where you go, you will always be the child of my heart.

A LETTER TO READERS

Dear Reader,

This book is set in the Deep South. As such, it contains a great deal of colorful, colloquial, and occasionally grammatically incorrect language. This is a deliberate choice on my part as an author to most accurately represent the region where I have lived my entire life. This book also contains swearing and pre-marital sex between the lead couple, as those things are part of the realistic lives of characters of this generation, and of many of my readers.

If any of these things are not your cup of

tea, please consider that you may not be the right audience for this book. There are scores of other books out there that are written with you in mind. In fact, I've got a list of some of my favorite authors who write on the sweeter side on my website at https://kaitnolan.com/on-the-sweeter-side/

If you choose to stick with me, I hope you enjoy!

Happy reading!

Kait

CHAPTER 1

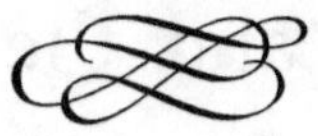

"THERE IS NO WAY I'm moving into your newlywed love shack."

Pru Reynolds froze, holding in a wince as the object of the current discussion made herself known. Of *course* Ari had been skulking outside the kitchen. How many times had Pru herself done the same as a child? There never seemed to be another option when the grown-ups were deciding your fate without consulting you. She'd hated it. Hated being at the mercy of a bunch of relative strangers—even well-intentioned ones. But that's what it was to be part of the foster system. That was the fate that Pru and her sister, Kennedy, were trying to save Ari from.

Pru turned to face the girl, taking in the dark, stormy eyes and the mulish set to her mouth. "Nothing's been decided, sugar. We aren't going to make that decision for you." It was important to get that out there. To make Ari understand that she had a choice here. Foster kids had so few actual choices, and fighting that sense of powerlessness was one of the biggest hurdles to overcome.

"Yeah," Kennedy added. "We were just re-viewing your options, discussing the pros and cons, so we could present them in a nice, orga-nized fashion."

Ari arched one eyebrow in a move that dis-played all of her barely teenaged disdain. Not yet fourteen, she was going to be a pistol, as their mother used to say.

Pru rode out the instant lash of pain at the thought of Joan. It had been just under four months since they'd lost her to a car accident.

Just under four months since she and her three sisters had taken charge of the girl Joan had been in the process of adopting. Joan had meant Ari to be one of them—the last and youngest Reynolds sister. But the legalities hadn't been finished, so Pru and Kennedy, and Kennedy's fiancé, Xander, had all undergone the necessary certification classes to serve as her foster parents. Not something Pru had expected to be doing at thirty—prospectively taking on a teenaged daughter. But she'd be damned if she'd let the girl go back into the system. Ari was family.

"Come on and sit down. We'll talk about this," Pru told her.

Ari crossed her arms, but she came over and plopped down at the big farmhouse table.

"Do you want tea?" Pru asked.

One shoulder lifted in a shrug. "Sure."

Pru moved to the stove and reminded herself that the attitude was better than the complete, withdrawn silence after Joan's death.

"So, here's the deal, kiddo," Kennedy began.

"The great state of Tennessee has officially declared Pru, me, and Xander fit as foster parents. Well, we've passed all the classes, anyway."

Pru pulled mugs from the cabinet and began to fill tea balls with the loose leaf black tea she favored. "The next step is the home study, so we have to let Mae know whether she'll be doing that on me or on Kennedy and Xander. All of us are more than willing, so it's your choice."

Their situation was highly unusual. Officially, they shouldn't have had Ari at all until all the certifications had been passed and the home study completed. But their mother had been a foster parent for more than twenty-five years and a social worker before that. Mae Bradley, Ari's case worker, had known Joan all that time, and on Joan's death, she'd pulled some strings with the powers that be, convincing them that it was in the best interest of the child to stay put with someone familiar. God bless small towns.

"You're getting married this weekend and going off on your honeymoon to Timbuktu—" Ari said.

"The UK," Kennedy corrected, smiling a little as Pru set a mug of tea in front of her.

"—and I'm not gonna be moving in when you get back and stepping all over your newlywed toes. I *like* you and Xander. Why would I do that to you? Congratulations, Mr. and Mrs. Kincaid. Welcome home! And oh, by the way, here's your teenager! That'd put an end to the honeymoon right quick."

Kennedy reached out to cover the girl's hand with her own. "Ari, Xander and I love you. It wouldn't be like that."

Ari pulled away, wrapping her hands around the mug Pru gave her. "You and Xander lost ten years. You deserve some time to be just together."

Pru couldn't argue with the truth of that. But it was Kennedy who'd first managed to pull Ari out of her shell after the funeral, so maybe she was the best sister for the job. Pru didn't care to analyze the pang she felt at that thought. "The home study will take some time. I expect, if you wanted it, Mae would be happy to do home studies on all of us. Then, you could stay with me, while the lovebirds have their time, and go to them when you felt like you were ready."

Ari was already shaking her head. "I want to stay here, with you. I want to keep my room and help with the inn." She dropped her gaze to her mug, jiggling the tea ball. When she spoke again, her voice was small. "You were there from the beginning, and I want to be a Reynolds, not a Kincaid."

Pru's throat went thick. She exchanged a glance with Kennedy, who nodded slightly. "Then that's what we'll do."

Ari looked up and the guarded hope on her face cut Pru to the bone. "Really? You'll really adopt me, like Joan was going to?"

It wasn't a decision she made lightly. She knew what it meant to be wanted, to have the stability of a good forever home. Joan had done that for her, for her sisters, and provided a safe place to land for countless others, over the years. Pru might not have any intention of stepping fully into her mother's shoes, but for this one child, she'd do whatever it took.

"If that's what you want, then yeah. I'd like that. I'd like that very much."

Ari grinned, her temper fading with the speed of a summer storm. "Then I guess I'll have to start working on calling you Mom."

The word hit Pru in the chest like a sucker punch. Mom. She was going to be a mom. This was going to be her daughter. She was going to be fully responsible for another person's... everything. Holy crap.

"It'll take us both some getting used to," she managed.

Ari slid off the bench and came around the table to give Pru a quick hug. She wasn't touch shy like so many kids Pru had known, so Pru gave her a hearty squeeze, as her own mother would have done. Over the girl's thin shoulder, she saw Kennedy beaming.

"Just to try out my mom voice, have you done your sweep of the guest rooms to see if any of the TP or linens or complimentary toiletries need restocking before the next guests arrive?"

"Not yet."

"Hop to. The Johnsons are supposed to be here by six-thirty."

Ari saluted and scurried off.

"Congratulations, Mom. And you even did it without the baby weight," Kennedy teased.

Pru sagged back in her chair. "Jesus."

Her sister sobered. "Are you really okay with this?"

"Yes. I wouldn't have told her I'd do it, if I wasn't. I'm just…a little overwhelmed." And a little bit jealous that she'd be doing this alone.

Oh, Kennedy and Xander would help out. So would her other sisters, Athena and Maggie, whenever they were in town. But there'd be no husband helping her share the load or the joys. She envied Kennedy that. She'd assumed she'd meet someone eventually, but Eden's Ridge was a tiny town, with a shallow dating pool. Unlike her sisters, she hadn't left, other than to finish her training as a massage therapist. Eden's

Ridge was home. She'd found no grand passion here, and up until they'd begun planning Kennedy's whirlwind wedding, Pru had been fine with that.

She'd be fine with it again. Her mother had led a full and rich life without partner. She could do the same. If she felt a twinge of self-pity at that, she shoved it away. Ari was the priority. Taking care of her was what Joan would have wanted.

"It's a big step," Kennedy said. "I'd be worried if you didn't feel a little overwhelmed."

"That's probably been a little exacerbated by the fact that we've planned your wedding in a month. Thank God for Cayla Black." A friend from high school, Cayla was divorced and back in the Ridge with her four-year-old daughter, trying to get an event planning business off the ground. She'd jumped at the chance to use Kennedy as a guinea pig.

"She is, indeed, awesome," Kennedy concurred. "I don't even think Maggie could've done better."

"It helps that you don't care too much about the details beyond being married to Xander in the end."

"True enough. Speaking of, I want to swing by the house to see my other half before I head into work for the night." She rose and came around to hug Pru herself. "Mom would love that you're doing this for Ari."

"I know. And it helps a little bit. She feels kind of like a last piece of Mom."

"Are you gonna call Maggie and Athena to tell them the news?"

"They'll be here in two days for wedding festivities. I'll tell them in person. Go forth and squeeze in whatever canoodling you can manage."

Kennedy rolled her eyes. "Canoodling. You sound like Ari."

"Fitting since she's going to be mine." Pru felt another flutter in her belly. That would stop being scary at some point, right?

"Touché. Love you, Pru."

"Love you back."

When she was gone, Pru took their tea—now cold—and dumped it out. She popped her own into the microwave, then carried the mug back to her room. Formerly her mother's room. She'd moved in formally after she and her sisters had converted the old Victorian into a bed and breakfast to save the family estate. It was a long way from profitable yet, but they'd had steady bookings since they opened Memorial Day weekend and plenty more that stretched out well into the fall.

Sinking down into the overstuffed chair, she tugged open the drawer and pulled out the photo album with "My Kids" embossed across the front. She'd found it in the course of cleaning out. This book contained photos of every single child her mother had fostered over the years. There were so many.

Had her mother felt this bone deep panic at the beginning? Wondering whether she could do this? Whether she'd irrevocably mess these kids up? Or had she always been the unflappable, down-to-earth woman Pru remembered? With the weight of the decision she'd just made pressing down, she needed her mother's comfort. So, tea in hand, she opened the cover and slid into memory.

"What's the status update on the wedding?"

"For God's sake, Maggie, we've been here all of five minutes. Can't you wait to try to run things until we've had some time to breathe?" Athena complained.

Maggie shot her a cool look. "The wedding is in five days. There's no time to relax."

And my sisters are officially home, Pru thought.

"We hired a wedding planner. And Pru's here. Shit's being handled. Right?" Athena looked to Pru for confirmation.

Her lips twitched. "Shit is, indeed, being handled." That her sisters trusted her to do exactly that was both flattering and maddening.

"See there? Now relax, woman." Athena flopped down on the overstuffed sofa.

"Might I remind you that there are little ears present, so perhaps tone things down from the language you use in your restaurant kitchen?" Pru suggested.

Ari and Athena both rolled their eyes.

"Gordon Ramsey is worse," Ari said. When Pru arched a brow, she just shrugged. "What? I really like *Kitchen Nightmares*."

There was no need to ask who got her hooked on that.

"Oh, did you see that episode with that poser in Ohio?" Athena asked.

"'I can cook, Joe,'" Ari said, in a passable parody of the celebrity chef.

"That was *brutal*," Athena agreed.

"Well deserved," Ari pronounced.

Deciding she was just grateful the two were bonding, Pru turned her attention to Maggie. "To answer your question, everything is going fine. Our bridesmaid dresses are ready and waiting. You and Athena have your final fitting tomorrow. The photographer is lined up, and Mrs. Lowrey, from church, is making the cake."

"You're not doing the cake?" Ari asked Athena.

"I'm a chef, not a baker. I *can* bake. I choose not to."

"Plus, Mrs. Lowrey makes the *best* red velvet cake in the state," Kennedy announced, sailing into the room with a tray of drinks from the kitchen. "She has a blue ribbon from the state fair that says so."

"What about music?" Maggie asked.

"My friend, Flynn, will be playing."

"Oh, did you finally talk to him about it?" Pru had heard plenty about the Irish musician Kennedy had toured with for a while, during her time abroad. He'd been one of the first to book a room after they opened the inn.

"No. He's playing his way down the East coast. Not quite sure where he is just now, and his cell phone doesn't work in the States. But he'll be here in a couple of days. It's not like he's going to say no. It's my *wedding*."

Maggie pinched the bridge of her nose and moved her mouth in something that might have been a silent prayer or a curse. "Okay, so what's left?"

"Just decorating the barn for the ceremony and getting tables set up for the reception. And we'll have help with that. Everybody who's got a room booked from tomorrow through the weekend is one of Mom's former fosters. And there are more coming in day of," Pru told her.

Maggie's shoulders relaxed a little. Kennedy swung an arm around them. "Did you think you were going to have to wade in and sort out chaos?"

"It wouldn't be the first time. But I should have known better. I can always rely on Pru to have my back." She flashed a grateful smile.

Pru just shrugged. "It's what I do."

"Is there anything else I need to know about?"

From the sofa, Ari began to bounce.

"You got ants in your pants, kid?" Athena asked.

Ari looked at Pru, and it was impossible to hold back the smile.

"She's excited because she's finally going to be a Reynolds. I'm adopting her."

"Whoa." Athena hooked Ari around the neck and pulled her into a headlock. "Welcome to the family, kid."

Maggie smiled at the giggling teen, who was digging her fingers into Athena's sides in a vain effort to tickle her. "That's wonderful."

"There are still some steps to go through, but that's the plan," Pru said.

The doorbell rang.

"Are we expecting more guests?" Kennedy asked. "I didn't think we had anybody else booked for tonight."

"Not guests. Your surprise," Pru said. "Ari, you want to go get the door?"

"'Kay!" Red-faced and gasping, she rolled off the sofa and raced out of the room. Moments later, she came back, a smiling blonde in tow.

"Hail, hail, the gang's all here," the blonde called. "Welcome home, y'all."

"Abbey Whittaker! I had no idea you were back in the Ridge." Maggie crossed the room to give her a hug.

"Only been back a couple of weeks. Granddaddy Whittaker isn't doing so great. His dementia is getting worse, so I came back to help out, while the family figures out what to do about it."

"I'm so sorry to hear that. But I'm definitely glad to see you. Weren't you off in Atlanta?"

"That's where I headed when Pru and I finished school, but I wound up moving to Mississippi last year. I've got kin in Wishful—Granddaddy's brother and his branch of the family are there. I've been working at a swank spa in Wishful."

"Which is why she's here tonight," Pru said. "She's giving all of us spa treatments."

"All natural and guaranteed to rejuvenate and relax."

Athena jerked a thumb at Maggie. "This one definitely needs to relax."

Abbey laughed. "And what about the bride to be?"

"Pretty sure she's the most laid back one here," Pru said.

"She's in luuuuuurve," Ari sang.

"It shows. Hard to duplicate that kind of glow with even the best products. You look great."

Kennedy beamed. "Thanks. Being happy agrees with me."

"The regular nookie doesn't hurt," Athena added.

Pru clapped her hands over Ari's ears. "Athena!"

"What? It's true."

Ari tugged the hands away. "Joan already had the talk with me. Great sex between mature, committed individuals is good for your mental health."

Pru's mouth fell open, but nothing came out. Her face felt frozen somewhere between horror and laughter.

"Well, she's not wrong," Kennedy admitted.

Maybe that's what's wrong with me. No great sex in.... Have I ever had truly great sex? When was the last time I had even mediocre sex? Oh, dear God, why am I thinking about this now?

Cheeks burning, Pru looked at Abbey, who was valiantly trying not to snicker. "Our mom was really big on female empowerment. But for you, young lady, that can wait until you're twenty-five." She grabbed Ari by the shoulders and marched her toward the kitchen, laughter in their wake as everyone trailed behind.

Abbey unloaded the bags she'd brought and began mixing ingredients, while Kennedy rounded up a bunch of towels. As she created multiple bowls of fragrant glop, Abbey scanned them all. "So, other than the bride, who else is tripping down the relationship highway? Or dating? Or anything involving the prospect of a significant other? Because I most definitely am not, and I need to live vicariously through somebody."

"Those Mississippi boys not doing it for you?" Athena asked.

"There's one very serious problem with them—it seems all the good ones are taken."

"It's a definite problem in small towns," Pru agreed. "I can't remember the last time I had a date."

"Didn't you go out with Gavin Harkness around Christmas?" Maggie asked.

"I went to dinner with him. For what I *thought* was just a meal between joint committee members for that Angel Tree fundraiser. I didn't realize he thought it was a date until he tried to kiss me when he brought me home. I turned my face at the last second and he hit my cheek. Then he just kind of froze there for several seconds, until I managed to twist the doorknob and escape. It was…awkward."

"Well, it's not like the city is any better for prospects," Maggie said. "In L.A., everybody meets people with an eye for how they can be used to further their career. There's no such thing as a simple girl meets guy on an elevator and gets asked to dinner, for a night of conversation about mutual interests. Instead, he's asking enough questions during the salad course, you feel like you're in the middle of a job interview."

Abbey grimaced. "That sounds awful. Please tell me you skipped dessert."

"I gave serious thought to disappearing to the bathroom and never coming back. But he knew my boss, as it turns out, so I stuck it out."

"What about you, Athena?" Abbey asked.

"I intimidate men."

"Shocker," Kennedy murmured.

The impact of the middle finger Athena shot up was somewhat mitigated by the bright green avocado mask smeared all over her face.

"So, other than the bride, we're all failing in the dating department. Y'all, this is a sad state of affairs. We are smart, sexy, available women. What is wrong with all these men?" Abbey came back to the table, passing out warm, wet wash cloths. "Everybody wipe off your mask with firm, downward strokes from the center line of your face."

Kennedy rubbed at the bentonite clay mask

already flaking off her face. "Maybe I should hook y'all up with some of Xander's single friends. All of his groomsmen are available."

"Please," Athena snorted. "Porter was one of our brothers."

"That still leaves Logan and Jonah," Kennedy pointed out.

"Athena and I don't live here, so that seems a pointless effort. But maybe one of them would suit Pru." Maggie angled her head, studying Pru from across the table.

"Hello, I'm sitting right here and *not* looking for a setup, thanks very much. I do not need a pity date. I haven't even thought about dating —" She cut herself off before *since Mom died* could spill out. No reason to drag the group down. "Besides, I've got enough on my plate with the inn and the fact that I'm acquiring a teenager."

"Yeah, but at least I came housebroken," Ari said.

"Girl's got a point. Men are so much harder

to train than dogs," Athena agreed. She patted her face dry. "Dude, my skin feels amazing."

"Mine's all tingly," Maggie said.

Abbey set a small bowl on the table. "Here, each of you slather some of this on. It's specially made moisturizer. No chemicals."

"It feels wonderful. All of it does," Pru said. "You know, a lot of my massage clients would love this. What would you think about doing some freelance spa treatments, while you're here? We could set up some space for you to work out of."

"That would be wonderful. The Babylon is holding my job, but it would be great to keep my hand in things. Plus, I'll need a break from Granddaddy."

"Great. We'll set a time after the wedding to discuss terms."

"Sounds like a plan." Abbey removed the double boiler she'd had simmering at the stove. "Now, who wants a paraffin bath for your hands?"

~

FLYNN BOHANNON LIVED a gypsy's life, traveling from town to town, venue to venue, sharing the music of his homeland. To his way of thinking, there was nothing better than seeing new faces, new places, every few days. If things began to feel a little stale, he picked up stakes and found somewhere new. Sometimes he traveled in a group, jamming with other musicians he met along the way. Other times, like now, he was a solo act. Either worked fine for him. It was all about the music.

He'd landed in Boston three weeks before and had been working his way down the Eastern seaboard, playing in pubs, bars, taverns, and coffee shops—a different town or city every night. Some shows had been pre-booked. Others, like the pick-up session he'd had in that pub in Baltimore, where the bartender had turned out to be the cousin of a friend of his mother's, had been a delightful, impulsive surprise. Flynn liked surprises. Which was why he'd made his way to Eden's Ridge, Tennessee a day early.

He'd wanted to surprise one of his dearest friends. And, he admitted, he hoped to catch her before she'd put on her *everything's fine* face and get a real read on how she was doing. Kennedy Reynolds had been every bit the gypsy he was, and now she'd come home and decided to settle here out of family obligation. Not that he frowned on that. There was a child involved. But he wondered how long it would take her to feel choked by the roots she'd long ago escaped.

It was beautiful. He'd give her that. These were younger, wilder mountains than he was used to. There simply weren't this many trees in the mountains of Ireland. At home, the peaks had been whittled down by wind and weather and time, until they'd been reduced to their bare essentials. Wild, yes, but often barren but for the grasses and scrub. Here the trees stretched in a lush, green blanket as far as the eye could see. As he navigated the switchbacks, he noted the craggy rocks peeking through here and there, but otherwise, everything was alive with the vibrant colors of summer.

The house was set back in the trees, a charming Victorian painted a mystical greenish gray, with crisp, white trim. He'd have recognized it from Kennedy's description, even without the wooden sign above the porch proclaiming The Misfit Inn. It rose a towering three stories high, with a turret to one side. The porch wrapped all the way round, with fanciful scrollwork at the corners and various groupings of chairs or gliders set to take in the view, which was magnificent from nearly all angles. There was the old bodock tree Kennedy had used to sneak in and out of the house as a girl. And beyond it, the barn, doors thrown wide.

Flynn found a place to park and climbed out. He knocked on the big front door, and when no one answered, he circled around back, scanning for Kennedy's familiar blonde head. He followed sounds of music—a cheerful country tune about some lass calling dibs—into the barn. The space inside was clear. White drapes had been hung above to block off what he presumed was a hay loft. Dozens of folding chairs were stacked to one side. And in the center of the barn, at the top of a ladder, a woman stretched to wrap white twinkle lights around a barn rafter. As he stood, undetected, she joined in the chorus with cheerful alto.

Charmed, he stayed where he was, watching. She was all soft curves, a fact made evident by the stretch of shorts across her perfect, lush backside. Flynn took a moment of reverence for that magnificent ass, captivated by the gentle flex of it as she worked and twitched her hips to the rhythm on the radio. *Now* that *is a woman.* He'd know, as he'd made quite the study of them the world over.

The ass ended in tanned legs and sport sandals. Stifling an appreciative murmur, Flynn lifted his gaze higher, noting the swatch of olive skin between the waistband of her shorts and the t-shirt riding high as she reached to continue the wrap. He realized then that she was far too short to be doing this. She'd gone above that last safety step of the ladder trying to reach the beam well above her head. Even as he thought to speak up, the ladder began to wobble. The woman sucked in a breath, flailing for any kind of purchase.

Flynn leapt forward as the ladder toppled and the woman screamed. He didn't exactly catch her so much as break her fall, but he managed to wrap his arms around her as she crashed down, softening the impact as they both hit the ground. They both lay there, stunned, wrapped in a tangle. As she lifted her head and trained those wide, dark eyes on his, Flynn couldn't help but think his breathlessness and pounding heart weren't entirely from the collision.

I'm callin' dibs, indeed.

He couldn't stop himself from reaching out to brush the hair back from that exquisite face. "Are you all right, then?"

"Flynn?"

Well, and wasn't it a fine thing to hear his name on those lips, in that soft Southern twang? As if she'd been waiting just for him, for this moment. The sound of it did something to him, plucking some chord deep in his soul until it sang. Could she feel it where her hands pressed against his chest?

"You're early," she said.

"Seems to me, I'm right on time."

Her pupils sprang wide at that, and she sucked in a breath. His gaze dropped to those lips, and his hand tightened at the curve of her waist. Only the sound of running footsteps kept him from leaning in to taste her.

"I heard a crash. What—Oh my God, Pru, are you okay?"

Pru. Which made her Kennedy's eldest sister.

Christ. He needed to get ahold of himself. Flynn relaxed his grip and leaned back. Seeming to collect herself, Pru shifted from his lap—more was the pity—and reached up to take the offered hand. That was when he realized the owner of the hand was a young girl.

"I'm fine. The ladder tipped."

The girl, who had to be Ari, looked down at him with bright, curious eyes. "Who'd you land on?"

Flynn rolled to his feet, offering his hand, as more people came into the barn, including the familiar face he'd come looking for.

"Flynn Bohannon!"

He grinned and opened his arms wide. When Kennedy leapt into them, he swung her in a circle. "It's good to see you, *deifiúr beag.*"

"Back atcha, boy-o! We weren't expecting you until tomorrow."

"I thought I'd surprise you. But I seem to have interrupted some sort of festivities. Are you getting ready for a party, then?"

"Oh, yeah, about that. There's someone I want you to meet." Kennedy pulled back and held her hand out to a broad-shouldered man, with close-cropped brown hair and a steady gaze. He slid his arm around her shoulders, and she looked up at him with absolute adoration. "Xander, this is my brother from another mother, Flynn. Flynn, Xander Kincaid, my fiancé."

Flynn's mouth fell open. "Your what now?"

Kennedy laughed. "It's our wedding we're decorating for. We're getting married on Saturday."

"Married?" Flynn repeated. Was she insane? She'd been home, what, four months? If that.

She laughed again, fairly glowing with happiness. "It's a long story, and I'll tell you all about it over a pint later. First, I want you to meet my family. This is Ari." She laid her hands on the shoulders of the young Hispanic girl, with the dark, soulful eyes and ready grin.

"Pleased to meet you," Flynn said, shaking her hand.

"And this is Pru."

"We've met," they said in unison.

Kennedy arched her brows.

"She fell out of the sky," Flynn said.

"More properly, I fell off a ladder," Pru corrected. "Thanks for saving me from breaking my neck."

He mimed doffing a hat and bowed. "Happy to be of service, milady. Perhaps you'll let someone taller assist you in finishing with the lights?"

Pru flushed. "Oh, you're a guest. I'm not—oh my God, your room's not ready." She looked, if possible, even more flustered by that than she had crashing into him.

She was already turning toward the door, when Flynn caught her hand. "It's fine. Don't trouble on my account. I arrived early and unannounced. Just shove me in a closet or something. I'll be fine." That sent his mind off on a merry little jaunt, imagining what it would be like to drag Pru into a linen closet and get to know the rest of those lovely curves.

She looked scandalized, and he wondered if he'd said that aloud. Or maybe it was that he'd been rubbing circles on the back of her hand with his thumb.

"You're a guest at our inn. You'll have a proper room. Just give me fifteen minutes—twenty at the outside."

"Psh," Kennedy snorted. "He's family."

"The family all have beds," Pru argued.

Now was definitely *not* the time to suggest sharing hers. And really, he needed to quash this whole reaction. This was Kennedy's *sister*.

"Fine. You fix a room. *I'm* putting him to work. He and Xander can finish with the lights. Maggie and Athena should be back from their fitting soon, and it's Athena's turn to cook dinner."

Pru tugged her hand free and started for the door. "Fifteen minutes," she repeated. "Ari, come help me please."

Because he wanted to watch her go, Flynn deliberately turned toward the ladder and righted it. "Right. Lights?"

"To start." Kennedy grinned.

He propped an arm on one of the rungs and gave her the side eye. "Oh, so that's how it is? You're going to make me work for my supper?"

"I'm going to make you play for it. I want you to play for the wedding. Will you? I know it's last minute and all, but you're here and there's no one else I'd rather hear."

Flynn still wanted to know the story behind this sudden rush to the altar. But given her fiancé was watching him from ten feet away, he opted for the only safe answer. "I'd be honored."

Kennedy threw her arms around him in another, staggering hug. "Oh, thank you!"

"Anything for you. Now, where are the rest of these lights?"

CHAPTER 2

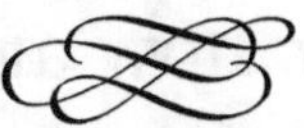

AFTER DINNER, ATHENA DECLARED dishes as someone else's responsibility and disappeared for a poker game with a couple of their foster siblings, who'd come to town for the wedding. Ari had gone up to watch, and Maggie holed up to do a little telecommuting for her firm in L.A. Wanting some quiet and a chance to find a little balance again, Pru shooed Kennedy and Flynn off to the family room for a visit. It seemed she hadn't been able to quite catch her breath since she fell off the ladder and into his arms.

What *was* it about accents that were so damned sexy?

She could hear Flynn's clearly from the family room as she washed and stacked. "Tell me true, *deifiúr beag,* how are you?" There was a wealth of affection in the term, and Pru wondered what it meant.

"I'm home," Kennedy said simply.

Flynn made a noise of disbelief. "You're as much a gypsy as me. You expect me to believe you're really okay with putting down roots again?"

"I enjoyed my travels, but you had me pegged that last night in Kerry. I was running."

"From Xander?"

"From mistakes. It's more complicated than that, but I'm in too good a mood to rehash all of it now. Suffice it to say, I don't have any reason to run anymore. I've loved him most of my life, Flynn."

"You're really happy here?"

"I really am. I've missed my family. I still want

to travel some, and I will for the book, but I don't feel the need to *go* anymore." She gave a contented sigh, and Pru could hear the smile in her voice when she spoke again. "Love will do that to you."

"And I suppose now you'll tell me I only need the love of a good woman?"

Pru figured a man like him must've had the love of more than a few. Because, damn, her long neglected lady parts were sitting up and taking notice. And unless she was very much mistaken, he'd taken some notice of her, too. Aside from the whole falling on him part.

Just what would it be like to have Flynn Bohannon in her bed?

Even as the thought formed, she pushed it away again. He wasn't her type. He was charismatic and gorgeous, with a serious case of wanderlust. A born heartbreaker. She'd loved a man like him once with all her heart, and he'd left her shattered and alone. Pru knew better than to expect anything else. Maybe, if she only had herself to think about, she'd consider it. But she was a mother now—or nearly. Her focus had to be Ari.

Still, it couldn't hurt to just look. Not looking at a man like him had to be illegal in some countries. Pru paused just beyond the threshold of the family room to do just that. He was so...well put together. He had a swimmer's build—long, lean limbs, with powerful arms, as she had reason enough to know. All that wavy, black hair fell into his eyes and just begged for fingers to run through it. Would it be as soft as it looked? What about the neatly trimmed beard? She'd never been a fan of beards before, but Flynn's worked, framing that strong jaw. Watching him in easy conversation with Kennedy, his bright blue eyes twinkling beneath a thick fringe of lashes—why were they always wasted on men?—she wondered if there'd ever been anything between them beyond friendship. There was no question that Kennedy had always been in love with Xander, but Flynn had seemed poleaxed at the announcement of her engagement. Was that because it seemed fast or because he thought there'd been a chance for something more?

"Are you really ready for this?" Flynn asked. "Isn't there anything else you want to do before you tie on the old ball and chain? Any carousing or adventures?"

Pru stepped into the room. "Considering she did most of her carousing with Xander…"

"True story," Kennedy admitted.

Flynn winced as he sat up, before his grin spread wide. "Kennedy Reynolds, were you a wild child?"

Kennedy feigned an innocent face.

Pru gave her the side eye before holding her thumb and forefinger a fraction of an inch apart.

Kennedy shrugged. "Well, maybe a little."

Pru zeroed in on the hand Flynn rubbed along his nape. "Are you hurt?" Had she injured the poor man by falling on him?

"What? Oh, no. I'm just all kinked from the car. It'll go away in a day or two."

"Pru can fix that. She's a massage therapist. You should let her work on you."

That benign statement sent Pru's brain skittering down a path that involved Flynn, naked on her table, with nothing but a sheet covering that magnificent—

"Well, if you think you can sort out this knot before bed, I'd probably sleep better for it."

Pru blinked. "Sure, I can do that. It's the least I can do for crashing into you."

"Better me than the ground. It would hardly do for the maid of honor to break a leg days before the wedding. Where do you want me?"

Anywhere I can get you. The thought bloomed before she could stop it, along with heat in her cheeks. "Um…"

"Should I sit or lie down?"

For the massage, you sex-starved idiot. Get a grip.

"I'll see what I can do here, and if you need something further, I'll get you on my table. Move over to the ottoman."

He complied, scooting to the back edge as

instructed.

Rubbing her hands together to warm them, Pru moved behind him. She considered asking him to take off his shirt, but given the direction of her thoughts, that seemed like a bad idea waiting to happen.

I am a professional, damn it.

Determined, she laid her hands on his shoulders, switching into professional mode and analyzing his muscles by touch, searching out the size and shape of the knots, finding their edges.

"So, Pru, what will it take to bribe you into sharing stories? I feel like I need to hear about Kennedy the wild child."

"Oh, I'm not sure even you are that charming," she teased.

"Is that a challenge, Miss Reynolds?" He tipped his head back to meet her eyes and his hair brushed over her hands. Yeah, soft as it looked.

Pru's pulse jumped.

A professional charmer, she reminded herself,

digging into the knots. *Better to steer clear.*

"Not even your blarney can overcome the sacred bonds of sisterhood," Kennedy announced.

Pru laughed. "Sure, let's go with that."

Her sister gave a mock glare. "It hardly matters anymore. Xander's reformed now that he's the sheriff." She grinned and gave a saucy wink. "Mostly."

"He's the sheriff?"

"Interim. But that's just until the formal election in November. He's going to win by a landslide."

"Sheriff or no, I bet you'd still be able to talk him into skinny dipping at Opal Springs," Pru said.

"Skinny dipping, is it now?" Flynn wanted to know, drawing out his Irish as he looked to Kennedy.

"No better way to spend a hot summer night," Kennedy said.

"I can think of a few." The words were out before Pru could stop them. She rushed to cover her gaffe. "But I'm pretty sure y'all had that covered, too."

Flynn's laughter was pure delight. "What about you, Pru? Did you ever take a walk on the wild side and swim in the buff?"

Kennedy answered for her. "No way. Pru is the good, responsible sister, who never stepped a toe out of line and made the rest of us look bad. We might have hated her a little for it, if not for the fact that she was also the one who covered our asses."

The good, responsible sister.

It was undeniably true. She'd lived her life following the rules. She liked rules. Liked order. Life ran smoother that way. So why did the teasing rankle?

"The poison ivy you got on your ass was hardly a motivation to follow your example," Pru countered.

Kennedy winced. "Okay, you make a good point. But thinking back to that summer…still gonna call it worth it."

Satisfied she'd mapped the problem areas,

Pru began to press and knead at Flynn's shoulders. She didn't have any memories like that. Of something reckless and fun that she could look back on to say she'd really lived. She'd always done the safe thing. She'd needed that after her childhood before Joan. Lord knew, now that she was taking on a child of her own, safe was the only option. And that thought was just a little bit depressing.

Beneath her hands, Flynn tensed, sucking in a breath before relaxing back against her with a groan of pure, unadulterated pleasure that had Pru's thoughts veering in a wholly unprofessional direction. "Jaysus, woman, where did you get those hands? That feels incredible."

The heat and strength of his back pressed against her front felt pretty incredible, too, and made her wonder all about the other ways she could get him loose and limber. And sweaty. She really wanted him sweaty.

"Told you she was good," Kennedy said.

Pru swallowed against a throat gone dry. "Better?"

"Much."

She stepped back. "Well, then. I'll leave you two to visit." She needed to get the hell out of here before she lost her apparently flimsy self-control.

Flynn rose and caught her hand as she started to move past. It was the second time he'd done that today, and it flustered her even more than she already was. He flashed her a devastating smile. "Thank you."

Two simple words, delivered in that unreasonably sexy brogue, left her weak in the knees. Then he lifted her hand to his lips, peering up at her through those thick lashes. "Hands this talented should be pampered," he said.

Christ almighty.

Digging deep, Pru managed to find a smile in return. "Nice try, but I'm still not telling you all of Kennedy's secrets."

Her sister hooted with laugher. Flynn straightened, wholly unabashed, and released her, but not before dragging his thumb down the center of her palm.

Heat flaring low in her belly, Pru made her escape.

~

"I DON'T THINK you understand how hen parties are supposed to work, love" Flynn observed. "The gents aren't supposed to be around for it."

"Psh." Kennedy waved that off and knocked back a shot of whiskey. "We're short on time, and there aren't that many places to *have* a bachelor or bachelorette party. It just made sense to do it together. Besides, I feel bad enough that I'm getting married and leaving town practically right after you got here to visit me. I wanted to spend what time I could with you."

"Fair enough." Flynn tossed back his own whiskey—not bad for not being Irish—and reached for her hand. "I know the bride is meant to be in charge, but if this is all the time I have with you, we're going to dance."

Grinning, she slapped her hand in his. "Yes,

we are! Denver!" She called to the bartender—also, apparently, her boss—who was regarding them both with amusement. "Queue up my playlist, will you?"

"You're the bride."

As they made their way to the empty space that had been cleared for dancing, the classic rock that had been playing low on the speakers stopped. A few moments later a lilting fiddle took its place.

"I might have planned for this eventuality," she explained, waving him to the opposite corner.

Flynn grinned. "Shall we show these Yanks how we do this in Ireland?"

In answer, she kicked her leg up and launched into a reel. He listened to the music for a few measures to get the beat, watching Kennedy circle the floor, her blonde hair bouncing and her face as light and joyful as he'd ever seen it. And no wonder, given the weight off her shoulders. They'd stayed up late the night before, and she'd filled him in on what had truly kept her away all these years. After all that, she and Xander deserved whatever happiness they could grab.

Flynn leapt into the dance, throwing himself into the familiar call and answer of dancing with a partner he knew well. They circled, their quick, rhythmic steps echoing off the wood floors. The assembled guests began to clap in time, cheering as each of them executed more and more complicated steps. By the time the reel was finished, they were both breathing hard and laughing. Kennedy's tiara was listing to one side.

They took their bows to much applause, and Flynn hauled her in for a hug and a smacking kiss on the cheek. "It's good to see you happy, *deifiúr beag.*"

"I've missed the hell out of you."

"Likewise. Now go dance with your groom. You've not taken your eyes off him since he walked in."

Beaming, she returned the kiss to Flynn's cheek and hurried over to Xander. Flynn himself headed for the bar and Pru. She wasn't drinking. He had no idea whether that was the norm for her or not. Everyone seemed to just know she'd be the designated driver. Since before they'd left the house, she'd been herding everyone else, making sure nothing was forgotten and everyone had a good time. Even as he approached, he overheard her speaking to Porter, one of Xander's groomsmen, "Go dance with Maggie before she sneaks away to the bathroom to check in with her office for the umpteenth time. Bonus points if you manage to steal her phone."

"Don't have to tell me twice." He saluted and cut smoothly through the crowd toward his target.

"Still taking care of everyone, I see."

"A mother's work is never done." She clearly meant it as a joke, but he heard something more serious in her tone.

"Ah, but you're not a mother yet."

She sipped at her tonic and lime. "Might as well be."

Which was sign enough that he ought to steer clear. He had rules for himself. But there was something about her that drew him, had him pushing, just a little. "Even so, mothers deserve to have fun themselves."

"Someone has to take care of everything." That someone was obviously her. How much of that was because she was the eldest and how much was because she was the sister who'd stayed?

"And who takes care of you?" It was something he'd been wondering since his arrival.

Her gaze flickered with surprise. "I take care of myself."

Flynn nodded, recognizing an independent woman when he saw one. He'd grown up in a house with two, hadn't he? The idea of somebody else taking care of her had never even crossed her mind. So he appointed himself—for the night, anyway—to make sure that she had a good time, too. He held out a hand. "Then come take care of me. I find myself without a dance partner."

"Oh no." Pru shook her head. "I can't do any of whatever you and Kennedy just did."

Flynn just flashed the grin that had a ninety-eight percent success rate. "I'll go easy on you." He angled his head, listening as the music changed. "See, there's something nice and slow." Which, in reality, was exactly what he'd wanted when asking Pru to dance. "C'mon. You won't leave a guest on the sidelines, will you?"

"You and I both know that, other than the bride, every woman in this room would be happy to dance with you. I'm pretty sure at least fifty percent of them started fanning themselves when they heard your accent."

True. American women did seem to fall all over themselves when he spoke. But not Pru. "Ah, but you're the only one I'm looking at."

Pink flooded her cheeks and she dropped her gaze.

To solve the issue, Flynn gently extracted the glass from her grip and set it on the bar. She didn't resist when he tugged her toward the dance floor. He slid his hand to the small of her back and pulled her into his arms, beginning to circle her to the bluesy, country guitar, as somebody sang about a woman and Tennessee whiskey. Pru's steps were a little stiff, her hold awkward.

"Relax. I won't bite," he said.

The fingers on his shoulder flexed, and he noted the pulse hammering in her throat as she lifted her gaze to his. "What if I ask nicely?" Her lips immediately pressed together and her color deepened, as if she hadn't meant to say that aloud.

Flynn's blood heated, and he shifted her an inch or two closer, angling his head to speak into her ear. "For you, *mo stór*, I would gladly do anything you ask."

A delicious shudder ran the length of her body. What would it be like to dismantle all those walls, stripping away her inhibitions until she came apart for him? The idea of it stirred him far too much.

"Even dishes?"

It was so out of sync with where his mind had gone, he pulled back slightly. "What?"

Pru laughed and her smile punched into him, strumming that internal chord he'd felt in the barn. "You did say anything."

"So I did." He didn't think he'd ever seduced a woman over a sink of dirty dishes. What would that look like?

"What does it mean?"

Her question distracted him from his little fantasy. A good thing, probably, given the crowd. "What does what mean?"

"*Mo stór.*"

"Ah. It's Gaelic for my darling."

Amusement quirked her lips. "Free with your endearments, are you?"

"I'm Irish," he said by way of explanation.

"What about that thing you keep calling Kennedy?" Was there a touch of prospective jealousy beneath that casual tone or did he just want there to be?

"*Deifiúr beag* means little sister, as she's been mine from the day we've met."

Her brows winged up. "Really? All these years and you two never…"

Flynn smiled. "No. I might have thought about it for about five minutes at the very beginning, but it was obvious her heart belonged to someone else. Now I know who."

They both looked across the dance floor to where Kennedy and Xander swayed, eyes only for each other.

Pru sighed, and he didn't miss the edge of sadness to her expression.

"Here now, what have I said to make you sad?" *Please don't say you've been carrying a torch for Xander yourself all these years.* He didn't know why that mattered so much, but it did.

"I just wish our mother was here to see them together like this. It was one of her greatest wishes that Kennedy would find her way home and back to him."

Flynn felt her tremble, saw her throat working against some strong emotion, and recognized the brittle armor she wore for everyone around her. He stepped back, pulling her with him. "Come on."

Pru blinked. "What?"

"Let's get a little air." He didn't wait for her assent before taking her hand and weaving through the patrons, to the door that led to the designated outdoor smoking area. No one was there, and he was grateful. She needed a few moments away from everyone who knew her. "There. Just breathe for a bit."

In the dim glow of the patio lights, tears glimmered in her eyes. "I'm sorry. I'm a little emotional."

Before she could do it herself, he gently wiped away the first one to escape. "We don't shy from emotion where I come from. If you need to cry, cry. I'll not think any less of you for it."

"I'll ruin my makeup."

"All right then. All joking and flirtation aside, maybe just take a minute to lean instead." He opened his arms.

Pru frowned. "You don't even know me."

"Consider me a shoulder by proxy. I've been one often enough for Kennedy over the years."

"You were there when I called her about Mom."

"I was." He'd held his friend, while her world shattered into a million pieces. "I don't know what it was like for you in the days and weeks after Joan's death, but I get the feeling you've been too busy being the shoulder for everyone else to take some support yourself."

She hesitated, as if not at all certain what to make of him.

"No judgment. No strings. Sometimes you just need to be held."

As another tear slid down her cheek, Pru stepped into him. Flynn wrapped her tight. She laid her head against his chest and released a bone-weary sigh. He said nothing as her body relaxed by degrees against his, just slid one hand beneath her hair and gently massaged her nape.

"I thought I was all cried out. But, God, I miss her so much right now, I can barely breathe."

"You and your sisters would have imagined her at all your weddings and births and other milestones. It's natural to feel the ache that she's not here in body to share in the joy."

"I need to get a handle on this, at least until after the wedding. I won't let anything spoil Kennedy's day."

"Letting yourself be human won't spoil anything."

"I don't get to be human. I'm the glue. The mediator. Jesus, I'm about to be the actual mom —which is scary as hell. And I wouldn't *not* do that. I love that child. But sometimes it's all just…"

"A lot?"

She sighed again. "Yeah."

"You know what I think?"

"I expect you'll tell me." Her tone held a faint smile.

"I think your mother would be proud of everything you've done, but that she wouldn't expect you to fill her shoes. So maybe instead of trying to be all things for everyone, remember you just have to be Pru, and she's pretty amazing all on her own."

She lifted her head to look up at him. "And you would know that how?"

"I've got eyes."

In another time, in another place, he might have kissed her then. God knew, he wanted to. But that wasn't what she needed.

"You're really good at this whole shoulder, thing." Her vague look of suspicion as she said it told him he'd made the right call.

"I've known my share of strong women who need one from time to time."

"Nice to know you're more than a pretty face and blarney."

Flynn batted his eyelashes and put on his best coquettish expression. "You think I'm pretty?"

Laughter cleared the last of the shadows from her eyes, and she stepped back just as the door opened and someone came out.

Xander eyed them both with that cool-eyed cop stare. "You okay, Pru?"

"Fine. Just needed some air." She turned to go back inside, but shot a look over her shoulder. "Thanks, Flynn."

"Anytime, *mo stór.*"

She smiled and went back to the party.

Xander stayed where he was, studying Flynn. "Watch your step, pal. Pru isn't for playing with."

The warning made Flynn like him more. "You'd be the brother figure, then." He nodded. "Good. She needs someone looking out for her." After this week, that someone wouldn't be him. The idea of that gave him an odd little twinge.

"Kennedy's told me about your reputation with women."

"I'm not looking to make a conquest. You've nothing to worry about. Besides, your focus should be on your bride. Because if you don't make her happy, I'll break you in two." He slapped Xander on the shoulder and went back into the tavern.

CHAPTER 3

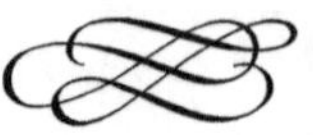

$\mathcal{P}$RU CRIED AT THE wedding. At least she was wearing waterproof mascara tonight. In her defense, she always cried at weddings, but this time she simply couldn't contain her joy that Kennedy and Xander had finally made it to where they were meant to be years ago. It gave her hope that the forever kind of love did exist.

As she watched them exchange rings beneath a gorgeous, hand-carved arbor, twined in flowers, envy lanced through her for the briefest of moments. She wanted that for herself, wanted a man to look at her with those star-struck eyes and promises on his lips. That probably wasn't in the cards for her. Her life was taking a different track because of Ari, and she was okay with that. But Pru couldn't shake the sense of a door closing on this chapter of her life. The child had to come first. Ari needed to *know* she was the priority after years of uncertainty from her family of origin. Pru didn't balk at that. She understood that need from deep, personal experience. But thinking back to her conversation with Flynn the other night, she wondered when she'd next have an opportunity to think about herself first.

She looked past the bride and groom to find him watching her and felt a long, liquid pull in her belly. What if now was her last chance? Shouldn't she seize it with both hands?

"I now pronounce you husband and wife. You may kiss the bride."

Pru tore her attention back to the happy couple just as Xander dipped his wife low, taking her mouth with his. Everybody cheered. Her eyes found Flynn's again, as he lifted his fiddle to play the recessional. Those bold blue eyes followed her, along with his cheerful music, as she took Porter's arm and trailed the newlyweds out of the barn. She felt the weight of his gaze, as she suffered through pictures in the boots she couldn't wait to shed. And she thought of him while she made a quick trip through the kitchen and got run out by Athena, as she snapped orders to the crew she'd brought in from her own restaurant for the day. Pru mingled, moving from guest to guest, to make certain everyone had what they needed, playing perfect hostess. All the while, awareness hummed along her skin, and she wrestled with what to do about it, considering consequences and benefits, as she'd done all her life. It distracted her through most of the speeches, until she heard her own name mentioned.

"As the only one with sense among us, Pru managed to spirit the mascot out of school before we got caught and sentenced to God knows what by Principal Lloyd." Porter glanced her way. "How *did* you get that thing back to Pineville High? All these years, and you've never said."

"I drove to Johnson City and mailed it back with no return address." Which any of them should've thought of, if they hadn't been so intent on causing mischief.

The crowd laughed and Porter lifted his glass. "Thank God for Pru."

Kennedy and Xander lifted theirs, along with the rest of the wedding party, and repeated his toast. "Thank God for Pru."

Thank God for Pru. Their well-intentioned words echoed through her head as they drank. *Thank God for Pru. The stable sister. The reliable sister. The one who will always be there, always put everyone else first. The one no one ever questions because she's never done one damned thing in her life to step a toe out of line.*

She gritted her teeth as she tipped back her own champagne.

Thank God for Pru. The boring, predictable sis-

ter, who has no life, so of course, we can count on her for everything.

She simmered about it through the rest of the speeches. She stewed during Kennedy and Xander's first dance. By the time the rest of the crowd flooded the dance floor, she'd made her decision. Pru Reynolds wasn't going to be the boring sister anymore. Not tonight, anyway.

She downed some of Denver's spiked lemonade and pushed back her chair.

A hand entered her field of vision. "Would you be ready for a dance, then?"

Pru smiled up at Flynn. "I definitely am." She placed her hand in his, devastatingly aware of the strength of his fingers curling around hers. If things went according to plan, she'd know a lot more about the feel of those hands before the night was through.

He lifted her hand to his lips. "You're beautiful."

Heat flooded her cheeks as she stared, transfixed, into the deep blue of his eyes. "You're charming."

Those eyes twinkled when he tugged her from her seat, and she wondered if he had dimples beneath the beard. As they stepped onto the dance floor, the music rolled over to David Gray. Flynn spun her into his arms and began to sway them both. Because she could, Pru relaxed against him, letting him lead and enjoying the heat of his body so close to hers.

"So the deed is done and everyone survived," he observed.

"I'm holding off on declaring the latter, until I see the number of hangovers in the morning. I expect more than one sore head by breakfast." There'd be mountains of breakfast to cook, no matter how little sleep she got, unless someone sweet talked Athena into kitchen duty.

"Easily dealt with. I know Kennedy's hangover remedy and can vouch for its efficacy."

"You may get called on to make it. But yes, the worst is over. Kennedy and Xander will be leaving for their honeymoon in the wee hours, and both Maggie and Athena are flying out tomorrow afternoon. The rest of our foster siblings will be heading out at some point tomorrow, as well." She braced herself. "I figure you won't be far behind, now that Kennedy will be off. Just so you know, we can shift your reservations around to come back later, when she's home."

"That's thoughtful, to be sure." He twirled Pru out and back, settling his arms more firmly around her. "I'll be here at least a couple more days, as I've no shows lined up for that span. I suppose you could put up with me on my own that long."

"That's not exactly a hardship."

His lips curved, drawing her attention. "Good."

Nerves she hadn't felt earlier kicked into high gear. She needed to put things in motion before she chickened out. She lifted her gaze back to his. "Flynn?"

"Mm?"

"Do you remember what you said to me when we danced the first time?"

For you, mo stór, *I would gladly do anything you asked.*

His pupils sprang wide. "I do."

She swallowed. "Did you mean it?"

"I did."

Oh, thank God. As the song drew to a close, Pru pressed closer, lifting her mouth toward his ear. "Then meet me in twenty minutes by the bench at the overlook in the back yard."

She didn't wait to see his reaction before walking away. If she was reading this all wrong, and he wasn't on the same page, she'd rather realize it in the dark by the overlook than look him in the face in a crowd.

The tempo of the music picked up. Pru threw herself into a line with her sisters for the Cha Cha Slide. She shook her groove thing with Ari for the Harlem Shake. She even threw caution to the wind and proved she still knew every move of the Macarena. The Chicken Dance was where she drew the line, stepping off the floor and heading for the bar. One of the other bartenders from Elvira's Tavern provided her with a second cup of the spiked lemonade. Ordinarily, she'd stop at one, but tonight was about pushing her limits and acting out of character. With one last glance around the floor—mostly to verify that all of her sisters and assorted foster siblings here for the wedding were occupied—Pru slipped out of the barn and into the night.

The air hummed with cicada song and crickets. This far into summer, night brought little relief from the heat. That made her plan all the more delicious. She crossed to the far side of the yard, watching for stray guests, but everyone, it seemed, was still packed into the barn. Good.

The overlook was empty.

Before Pru could process the disappointment of that, Flynn stepped free of the shadows.

Flooded with relief, she blurted, "You came."

"You asked." He reached out to skim his fingers along her cheek. "What do you want, Pru?"

She closed her eyes and leaned into the

touch, already feeling a trifle breathless. "I want to show you something. It's a bit of a walk."

"In the dark?"

"There's moonlight."

"So there is."

As she took his hand, Pru was conscious that he was letting her lead now. They left the yard, taking the trail she knew as well as she knew the house she'd grown up in. The sounds of the reception grew fainter as they went down the incline and wove their way through the trees. Neither of them spoke until the trees opened up some time later onto a small pool of water.

"This is Opal Springs."

It took Flynn a moment. "Of the skinny dipping story?"

"That would be the one."

"So this is where your sister got up to mischief. You've really never been?"

"No." She took a breath and met his eyes. "I was hoping you'd help me change that."

"Now?" The question escaped on a surprised laugh.

Pru looked out at the shimmering reflection of the moon in the water. "My life is about to change radically. This is the last time I get to think about myself first, and I don't want my headstone to say, 'Thank God for Pru. She was reliable.' So yeah. Now."

"Won't they miss us?"

She could still hear faint strains of music. "Not for a while yet. We might miss the cake cutting, but I really don't care."

Flynn stepped into her, sliding a hand along one hip. "Is it a swim you're after?"

Pru gripped his waist. "The swim is negotiable. I just want you."

"I JUST WANT YOU."

The four most beautiful words in the English language. They had Flynn wishing for a bed and privacy and time to fulfill her every fantasy and all of his. But she wasn't just any woman, ripe for a tumble. She was the sister of one of his closest friends. And she was not, as Xander had pointed out, for playing with.

Flynn wasn't feeling playful. None of the things Pru stirred in him were so simple as that. She was a woman who gave everything and asked almost nothing in return. Much as it seemed to rankle her, she *was* reliable and dependable—the family rock in the absence of their mother. But she was so much more than that and needed someone to show her. She wanted this, wanted him. How could he turn away from such a request?

He cradled her face, tipping it up until moonlight glimmered in the dark depths of her eyes. *"Ceann álainn."*

"What does that mean?" Pru murmured.

"Lovely one." Her cheek was exquisitely soft beneath his thumb. "And you are."

She turned her face into the touch and closed her eyes, his name a sigh on her lips.

He didn't know what she'd imagined when

she'd brought him down here. A fast, wet coupling in the spring? One night of hurried passion? He wanted to give her more than that. He wanted to take his time, wrapping her in layers of pleasure until she forgot all the stresses and heartaches she'd endured. So it was with gentleness he took her mouth, with tenderness he pulled her closer.

She melted into him, her body going pliant as wax against his. The instant surrender fired his blood, but he kept the pace slow and easy. She was a woman who deserved to be cherished. Flynn didn't want her thinking of a time clock or the inevitable end to whatever they brought to each other. He wanted her thinking only of his touch, his taste. Of the now. He traced the seam of her lips with his tongue. She opened for him, rising against him, her hands linking around his neck to pull him closer.

She tasted of the lemonade and of deeper, darker things, at odds with her usual sweet demeanor. Flynn sank into the taste of her, hauling her tighter against his body as need welled up to join with want, sparking urgency in his veins. And still he kept himself leashed, fought to maintain control. This was all for her. About her.

That was harder to remember as she wrapped one leg around his. He reached down, urging her leg higher, wrapping it tighter around him as he angled to press his erection into her hips. Pru whimpered, moving against him in a rhythm that made him half mad. He ran his hand up the warm, bare flesh, beneath the hem of her dress and higher, until he palmed that glorious ass. She moaned, pressing closer, until he was thinking three steps ahead, struggling to work through the logistics of getting her naked. Against a tree? God no. She deserved better that. But Jaysus, he needed some leverage.

There was a series of wide, flat rocks around the pool. Maybe he could get down on one. As the thought tried to form, he slid his hand lower, stroking over the silk between her legs to find it drenched.

Holy Mary, Mother of God.

Encouraged by her gasp, he nudged the silk aside and traced her bare flesh.

"Flynn!" Her cry was part shock, part demand.

He could do this, would do this, to give her pleasure and buy himself a little more time to think about how he was going to make love to her as she deserved out here, with no towels, no blankets, nothing to soften the ground. He slid one finger a scant inch inside her—

The snap of a breaking branch had him freezing.

"Wha—"

"Shh!" he hissed, listening.

Muffled voices had him hastily removing his hand, straightening her skirt. He tugged her into the trees, opposite the trail they'd come in on. They'd barely slipped out of sight before another couple came off the trail. The bridesmaid dress identified the woman as one of Pru's sisters. Athena? Who the hell was she with?

Athena turned toward the guy beside her.

"So how 'bout it, farmer boy? Are you up for a swim?"

"Is that a trick question?" The deep, rich voice sounded amused.

Pru gasped, "Logan?" She promptly clapped a hand over her own mouth.

But neither her sister nor Xander's other groomsman appeared to have heard a thing. They were both too intent on stripping down.

Flynn brought his mouth to Pru's ear. "Time to go."

As silently as possible, they picked their way through the trees, back to the trail. A splash of water and laughter made it evident Athena and Logan hadn't heard.

As soon as they were out of earshot, Pru blew out a breath. "I seriously may cry." She folded both arms across her middle, her face a mask of unsated misery.

Flynn adjusted his trousers, which were well past the point of uncomfortable. "Would it have been better if we *hadn't* heard them and they knew we were down there and why?"

"I don't know." She threw her head back and stared up at the sky. "God, I just wanted *one night*. Not even a full night. An *hour* for myself. And I can't even have that."

Her frustration was palpable, and it ripped at him.

Flynn caught her arm, turned her toward him. "You deserve far more than an hour."

"Yeah, well, the Universe disagrees." She gestured back toward Opal Springs.

"We have time. I'm not going anywhere just yet. And everyone else will be gone tomorrow."

"Ari won't."

"We'll figure something out," he promised.

"Sure." Pru turned away, clearly not believing him.

They headed back to the reception in silence, Flynn trying to come up with a plan the entire way. Parents had been having sex with children in the house since the beginning of time. There had to be a way to work this.

The party was still rocking and rolling, the crowd having barely thinned in their absence.

As they wove their way through the tables at the edges of the dance floor, Ari bounced over.

"There you are! You nearly missed *cake!*"

Pru smiled and wrapped an arm around the girl's thin shoulders. "That would be a tragedy, for sure. Let's go get some."

"I already had a piece," Ari admitted.

"Child, you only live once. If you want more cake, you can have more cake. Besides, Mrs. Lowrey won the state fair with this recipe five years running. It's worth two pieces."

Flynn watched as the two of them moved off toward the cake table, arms linked, dark heads bent toward one another. Something warm moved through his chest, seeing how easy they were together. Pru really was going to make a great mother.

By the time he made his way to the cake himself, another girl had bounded up. She gestured wildly with her hands, then the two girls turned pleading eyes on Pru, hands clasped in total adolescent supplication.

"Here now, what's going on?" he asked.

The second girl's eyes went wide at his accent. "You are *not* from around here."

"Indeed, I'm not." He grinned. "Is this begging for more cake? For I've not yet had my share."

"Your cake is safe," Pru assured him. "Kacy just invited Ari to go on a trip down to Nashville with her and her family. Tomorrow."

"I *know* it means me missing out on the cleanup after the wedding. But I swear I'll make it up with the rest of my chores around the inn. Please, Pru?"

"We'd only be gone a couple of days," Kacy added. "And I can help clean up when we get back."

Pru's face softened. "I want to have a word with Kacy's mom first to clear up some things, but you can go. You've worked quite hard enough the last few months to earn some time off."

Both girls whooped and practically knocked Pru over with their enthusiastic hugs. Then they were off again, racing, Flynn imagined, to tell Kacy's mom the good news.

He leaned in to get himself a slice of cake. "Seems the Universe had a backup plan after all."

CHAPTER 4

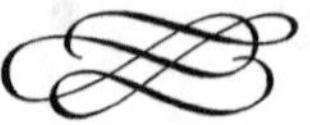

"DO YOU HAVE ALL your stuff?" Maggie asked Athena.

"I'm the one who's been standing down here with a fully-packed suitcase for half an hour." Athena eyed the stack of Maggie's luggage. "You never could travel light."

"Some of us had non-wedding related work to do while we were here."

And some of us have work to do after you go. But Pru didn't share that particular thought.

The house couldn't empty fast enough.

After she'd cooked what felt like the world's

largest breakfast—enough pancakes and sausage to feed the literal army under her roof—the first wave of her former foster siblings headed out. Right on their heels, Kacy and her parents had picked Ari up. Those who remained had helped with clean-up in the barn. The tables and chairs were folded and stacked, waiting for pick up by the rental company on Monday, and the other detritus from the reception had been swept up or cleared away. Mostly. The lights would take longer to pull down, but later. It could all wait for later. Pru just needed them all *gone* so she could have a minute or five to breathe. And maybc have a nap, since she didn't sleep a wink last night.

"Y'all should get on," she urged. "There's construction on I-40. You don't want to miss your flight."

"In a hurry to get rid of us, sis?" Athena's lips curved in the sort of loose, relaxed grin that only came from being thoroughly sated. Not that Pru would know anything about that since she hadn't been.

"Honestly, I want an afternoon of quiet where nobody wants anything from me. I've been going ninety miles an hour since we started the inn, and throwing Kennedy's wedding into the mix, on top of maintaining my own business, has meant no breaks for me." She came off harsher than she'd intended.

Maggie frowned. "The burden of the everyday running of things has absolutely fallen on you. That was never our intention. Maybe we should revisit the idea of hiring you some help."

"We can't afford it yet." It would be into the fall before they were truly in the black. "And it's fine. I'm just crabby and tired right now. Now that the wedding is over, things will slow down. Ari and I can manage fine, while Kennedy's away."

"What about Flynn?" Athena asked. "Is he sticking around now that Kennedy's off on her honeymoon?"

"He's here for a couple more days, while he lines up some new gigs. I expect he'll be gone by midweek, when the next reservations are booked." Pru refused to analyze the pang she felt at that.

"Where's he gotten off to?" Maggie looked around, as if just realizing Flynn had disappeared. "I haven't seen him since we finished with the barn."

"If he has any sense, he probably hid so we couldn't put him to more work. Now come on, you need to go, and I need to get started turning every room in the place. The laundry alone is going to take hours."

"Seriously, Pru, we can at least spring for some help while Kennedy's gone," Maggie insisted.

"If I need someone, I'm sure I can find someone. Now, I love you both, and I'm kicking you out." To solve the matter, Pru hugged each sister in turn and opened the door.

"We're going. We're going. Go have a nap," Athena suggested. "You'll feel better."

"I'll do that. Text me when you get back tonight."

They promised they would. Pru stood on the porch until they got the rental car loaded up and waved when they pulled out of the drive. As their taillights disappeared down the street, she shut the door, leaned back against it, and closed her eyes.

"Are they gone, then?" Flynn's voice came from the general direction of the stairs.

Pru exhaled a long breath. "They are. Thank you, baby Jesus."

She should really get started on those rooms, strip the beds, gather the towels… Even the thought of the remaining work made her want to curl up into a ball. But, of course, she shoved away from the door and started for the stairs.

Her phone vibrated with a text. Pru pulled it out to find a picture of Ari and Kacy strapped into…was that some kind of space shuttle simulator? The two of them were grinning and mugging for the camera.

Flynn peered over her shoulder. "Looks like she's having a good time."

"They're at the Discovery Center, I think. It's a science museum in Nashville." Pru blinked back sudden tears.

"Here now, what's wrong?" Flynn's arm came around her shoulders.

"I'm sorry. It's just, this is the first time she's asked to do *anything* away from us overnight since Mom died."

"I'm sure it doesn't mean she loves you any less."

"No, no. These are happy tears. It means she's feeling comfortable and safe. This is huge."

"You did that," he told her. "You and your sisters."

She turned into him, wrapping her arms around his waist and burrowing in because she needed to share this with someone. "That little girl means everything to me." Beyond being the last link to her mother, Ari was simply a joy.

"You're doing an amazing job with her." He ran a hand down her hair. "You're doing an amazing job with everything. Is there anything else you need to do right now?"

"I can think of at least a dozen things I should be doing."

"Things are all sorted with the wedding clean up. Give yourself some time."

Her heart began to pound as she realized that the house was, at last, empty and likely to stay that way for more than twenty-four hours. Nerves tumbled over themselves in her belly. It was one thing to proposition a man under the influence of alcohol and temper. But it was broad day and she was stone cold sober.

If Flynn noticed her nerves, he gave no indication. "Come on. I want to show you something." Tucking her hand in his, he led her up the stairs to his room on the third floor.

"Now that the inn has cleared out, we can move you to one of the bigger rooms."

"This one's fine." He opened the door and Pru went speechless.

There were candles—dozens of them—flickering from every corner. He'd rounded up some of the flowers from the wedding and scattered those around the room as well. Little pops of color and scent. She recognized the iPhone dock from the kitchen sitting on the dresser.

"Well," she managed. "Someone's been busy."

"I got into your stash of candles in the treatment room. I hope you don't mind. I wanted to set the stage."

Last night she'd thought to have some fun, get a quick release, and do something entirely out of character. But this was something else. Something more. And that was terrifying.

Flynn lifted her hands, kissed them. "I wanted you from the first moment I saw you."

Pru winced. "When I was hurtling down at you?"

His lips curved. "When I saw you up there on that ladder. Heard you singing."

"I don't have your voice."

"You've a perfectly charming voice. And a magnificent ass."

That surprised a laugh out of her. But nerves still tap danced in her blood. Because it seemed she could say anything to him, she gave them voice. "Flynn, I—It's been a very long time for me. And I've never been with anyone like you."

"Like me?"

"Someone who'd trouble with the trappings of romance. Who'd even think to set the stage for anything." Her previous lovers—and they'd been few—hadn't been quite so bad as wham, bam, roll over for sleep. But they'd been ordinary. Nothing about Flynn was ordinary.

"Then you've been with the wrong men." He turned her hands palm up and kissed the center, keeping those wild blue eyes on hers. "You're worth the effort and the time." He pressed his lips to the other palm. "And you deserve to be thoroughly seduced."

Moved, aroused, she could only stare at him. She'd wanted to do something for herself, to be selfish for once. What he offered was the most decadent indulgence she could imagine. And—for today, at least—there was no reason to stop. More, she didn't want to stop.

"Ari won't be back until dinner tomorrow,

and there are no new reservations until mid-week. We have the house entirely to ourselves."

He smiled. "Then let's make the most of it."

BECAUSE HE COULD SEE the nerves so near the surface, Flynn left her only long enough to turn on some music. To please himself and in hopes of relaxing her, he pulled Pru into a dance, circling her slowly as Erin Boheme crooned from the speakers. He liked how she fit with him, liked, too, how she ultimately relaxed into his lead. There was a trust in that. But this went so far beyond a dance. That she'd trusted him enough to ask for this, when asking was so very hard for her, humbled him. He intended to prove himself worthy.

Breathing in her scent, he pressed a soft kiss to her brow, lingering until he felt the tension there drain. Unhurried, he moved to her temple and down her cheek, repeating the simple brush of his lips, waiting for those tiny surrenders. Her head fell back on a sigh, exposing her throat so he could continue his gentle path downward. He murmured approval, encouragement, defaulting to Irish.

Sliding her hands beneath his t-shirt and up his back, Pru laughed a little. "I swear, you could read a grocery list in Gaelic and it would sound sexy."

Flynn smiled against her throat. "It's a language for flattery and curses."

He nudged the strap of her tank top down and found an intriguing hint of lace. "Let me see you, *ceann álainn.*"

She lifted the shirt off herself, letting it drop to the floor. Flynn drank her in, the sight of that smooth, olive skin against the black satin and lace of her bra.

"Were you wearing that earlier, while we were cleaning the barn?"

"I certainly haven't had a chance to change."

"Saints be praised." He traced the edge first with his finger, then gave in to temptation and followed with his tongue. Her shuddering breath lit all kinds of fire in his blood. He repeated the motion until her nipple tightened to a peak beneath the satin and took it into his mouth.

Pru's hands speared into his hair, holding him to her breast. He lingered there, suckling her through the fabric, as he busied his hands unhooking her shorts. He wanted to know if the underwear matched. Switching to the other breast, he drew the zipper down and eased them over her hips. Then he cursed reverently. The matching boy shorts were almost entirely lace, giving tantalizing hints of what lay beneath.

"If I'd known you were running around in something like this—Jaysus, woman. We'd have ended up naked in the hay loft."

"We wouldn't have been the first. Full disclosure—"

"Oh, we're getting there, to be sure."

Her throaty laugh underscored the music. "These aren't the norm. I wore them for you."

"Sure, and I have every intention of showing you how much I appreciate it."

He tugged his shirt off and moved in, grasping her by the hips and slanting his mouth over hers. Pru rose to him, wrapping around him and opening her mouth to his. Flynn's control slipped a notch at the taste of her. They pivoted, backing toward the high, four-poster bed. As lovely as the wrapping, he wanted what was underneath. With one hand, he flicked open the clasp at her back and drew the lace away. Her breasts were heavy in his palms, the nipples pearling beneath his touch. She moaned, reaching between them for the fly of his jeans. She had the zipper down almost before he could take another breath.

Flynn grabbed her wrist before she could snake her hand inside his boxers. "Wait."

In response, she twisted in his grip to bring their hands between them, urging him inside her panties.

"Does that feel like I want to wait?"

He cupped her, drawing a finger through

her wetness, until she dropped her head back on a curse that had his erection straining.

"God, it feels so good to be touched."

"We're only just getting started, love." Flynn brought her mouth back to his, as she began to move against his palm. It only took him moments to match her rhythm, adding a pressure that made her whimper. As tension began to coil through her again, he urged her higher, sliding in one finger, then two. "That's it, darlin', take your pleasure."

When she shattered on a scream, it was one of the most beautiful sounds he'd ever heard.

Pru clung to him, trembling. He kissed her gently, easing her back down from the crest, as he tipped her back onto the bed. She watched him from hooded eyes, while he shucked the rest of this clothes and climbed in after her. He moved up her body with long, lazy strokes of his hands, his tongue.

"Flynn?" Her voice held a little gasp as he nibbled at the sensitive flesh of her inner thigh.

"What?"

"That feels amazing."

He smiled against her skin. "Good."

"But if you don't hurry up and get inside me, I may have to kill you."

Flynn rested his chin on her hip and stared up the length of her body. "Is that the way of it then?"

"That is definitely the way of it."

"Well, then, as I value my life…" He leaned over to grab a condom from the bedside table, hurriedly protecting them both before settling in the cradle of her thighs. He searched her face. "All right?"

She reared up, hooking an arm around his shoulders and pressing her mouth to his. "Yes. Hurry."

Planting his arms on either side of her shoulders, he began the careful slide into her, watching those gorgeous eyes blur as he filled her. Her hands clamped on his shoulders and her legs tightened, her heels digging into his ass and pulling him flush with her body. She was tight and wet and so damned hot, he thought he'd lose his mind as he held still, giving her a chance to adjust.

She wriggled her hips, and he slid a little deeper. "Oh God, more. I need more."

Taking her mouth, he began to move, listening to her whimpers and moans, learning to play her body like a new instrument. And what an instrument. She matched his rhythm, shifting the angle of her hips to take him deeper, and he felt his control begin to fray.

She opened her eyes, cheeks and lips flushed with pleasure, and he thought she was the most beautiful woman he'd ever seen. He said as much, the words tumbling out in Irish, as he continued to move, to send her higher. She reached up, framing his face in her hands, and said his name. Just his name. And he felt something beyond arousal, beyond pleasure. A sense of homecoming he hadn't anticipated. It pulled at him, stealing his breath. Then she shattered, and the pulse of her release shot him over the edge, scattering his thoughts.

Flynn came back to himself listening to the

gradual slowing of Pru's breath. There was a comfort to the sound and to the feel of her in his arms. A peace he'd never felt with another lover. It was new and tantalizing, a drug he knew he'd be craving again, before he'd even forgotten the taste of her.

"I think I have to have this bed bronzed or something, so I can remember this moment after you leave." She sounded happy and sated, exactly as he'd planned.

Flynn drew lazy patterns on her shoulders. "I want to keep my existing reservation." The words popped out before he could think better of them, but he didn't want to pull them back.

Pru went very still before propping herself up to meet his eyes. "That's three more weeks."

Three more weeks—two of which Kennedy and Xander would be abroad. Three more weeks he could romance her as she deserved. "You said this was the last chance you had to take something for yourself. Why should you stop with one day?"

"Why would you do that?"

Flynn pulled her close again, brushed his lips over hers. "Because once would never be enough."

She hummed and stretched against him like a cat. "But what will you *do?* I mean, you have to work, don't you?"

"I will work. When I'm not actively performing, I write my own music. It's been some time since I've slowed down long enough for that. And, music aside, I'd like to help you with the inn."

Somewhere across the world, his sainted mother had just stopped to cross herself. But Flynn knew from long experience what it took to run such a place, and her doing it on her own, even with Ari's help, was a lot.

"Help with the inn?" She sounded utterly baffled by the suggestion.

"It's something I know a bit about."

"Being a professional guest is not the same as running things."

"To be sure. But my family runs a B and B in Clare, so I grew up turning rooms, scrubbing up, hauling luggage—with considerably less cheer about it than Ari does, I have to say."

"You grew up in a B and B?"

"I did. We had people from all over the world come through. I'd listen to them talk about where they were from and yearn to be the one out on the adventures instead of the one helping house the adventurers for the night. So, when I hit eighteen, I lit out to do exactly that and haven't looked back. But that doesn't mean I don't remember how it's done."

"That's sweet, Flynn, but you *are* here on vacation, and I'm not going to have you working, particularly not at something you didn't like doing in the first place. Besides, Kennedy says you get itchy being in one place for longer than a few days."

She wasn't wrong. Under normal circumstances, he'd be yearning for the road by now. But these weren't normal circumstances, and he found himself more content than he'd been in longer than he could remember. "Darlin', I've got no inclination to leave this spot for a century or so. And even then, it might be just for food."

Pru arched a brow. "And what, pray tell, would you *do* for a century?"

Grinning, Flynn rolled her beneath him. "Let me show you."

CHAPTER 5

"I KNEW I'D END up with a few clients from people I know, but word has spread like wildfire. Thanks." Abbey accepted the glass of wine Pru offered. "I've got more people wanting to book sessions than I can manage in the temp space we have set up right now. People here are really into the idea of a spa."

Balancing her own wine, Pru settled into one of the deck chairs opposite her friend. "I thought they might be." The news both pleased and worried her. She'd invited Abbey to ply her trade on a whim, a means of testing the waters. But she hadn't expected the idea to take off quite this fast.

"That's your thinking face. What's cooking in that brain of yours?" Abbey asked.

"I've been noodling over the idea of a day spa for a while. But I wanted time to gather some data on interest before I broached the subject with my sisters. A spa would necessitate renovations—an expansion or addition somehow. There's—"

The back door opened, pulling Pru's attention to the other end of the porch. She lost her train of thought as Flynn stepped out and grinned at her. Just that quick flash of his smile had her blood heating, and she had to fight not to grin foolishly back.

"Pru?" Abbey looked from her to Flynn.

Pru pokered up and prayed she wasn't blushing. Did she have a blinking neon sign over her head? *Having torrid affair with sexy Irishman.* "There's not room in the house for a full day spa without cannibalizing on guest space. Plus, I wouldn't want to have clients constantly tromping through and disturbing anybody. I mean, not that people tromp at a spa, usually, but you know what I mean."

"A day spa is it?" Flynn asked.

"Just brainstorming." Pru made introductions. "Abbey, here, has more business than she knows what to do with, and we're kinda straining at the seams regarding temporary space."

"And what is it you do?" he asked.

"Well, facials and aromatherapy is what I've been doing. Back in Mississippi, where my regular job is, I do body scrubs, wraps, and body masks, among other things. It's all about the pampering."

"That sounds grand. And you're thinking of introducing some of that here?"

"Eventually. I think the response Abbey's gotten has proved there's a local market, and certainly it's something guests would appreciate. But Abbey's only here temporarily, and we've only barely gotten the inn off the ground. We haven't yet made it solidly into the black from our initial start-up costs, so I can't hit my sisters up with the idea of investing more in an expansion without numbers to support it."

Flynn angled his head. "What if you did something on a smaller scale? You've already got the room for your massages. Couldn't you co-opt one of the guest rooms not being used? Temporarily transform it, while Abbey's here, gather your numbers. Now that the wedding's over, do you have any fully-booked weeks coming up?"

They didn't. They were getting a steady trickle of reservations, particularly for weekends, but during the week, reservations were still sparse. Pru considered. "What would you need, Abbey?"

"For what I'm already doing, just a comfortable reclining chair."

"What about the hydrotherapy and wraps and such?"

"Some of them require specialized equipment, but some could be managed with access to a bathroom with a tub and shower."

"How much time do you think you could manage away from your grandfather?"

"A fair bit. Mostly Mom has him during the day. It's evenings and nights I'm really helping out."

"I'd need to think on it, but maybe we could come up with something we could offer early in the week—maybe Tuesday through Thursdays? That wouldn't interfere with weekend room rentals and would give us a chance to turn over the room on Monday if someone was in it for the weekend. Day spa traffic could help offset costs when reservations are slow." The possibilities turned over in Pru's head. "Maggie will want concrete numbers. Some kind of temporary set up would allow us to test things and gauge interest for something more permanent. If I can prove to the rest of them that there's a legitimate market, then we could justify hiring someone else to do the actual running of the inn, and I can get back to massage."

"Well, I'm here for at least another month, so I'm game to try it out, if you are."

Pru was more than game. "Work up a list of possible services you think we can pull off here without having to purchase a lot of special equipment, and give me some estimates of the time for a session and what you'd charge. We'll see what we can hammer out that would benefit us both. And if you want to test out those products on some guinea pigs...we could maybe talk about sampler sizes that could be provided with the rooms or gift sets that could be sold."

"That is definitely something to think about." Abbey rose. "Thanks for the wine. I'm gonna be getting on. Gotta be getting dinner ready for Granddaddy. I'll get that list together tonight and bring it by tomorrow. Flynn, it was nice to meet you."

"And you as well."

Behind his back Abbey made an exaggerated *Oh my God!* face and fanned herself. Pru hid a smile in her wine. As Abbey got into her car,

Pru headed inside to figure out what they were having for supper themselves.

Flynn trailed behind. "Did you mean it, about running the inn?"

"Mean what?" She tugged open the door to the fridge and scanned the contents.

"Do you not like it, then?"

"I didn't ever have designs of being an innkeeper, no. I don't *dislike* it. And I don't mind it, especially as it's what's allowing us to keep our home. But with all the wedding planning and such, the actual management of it has landed a lot more on my shoulders than I'd expected."

When he reached up and began to knead at those shoulders, she moaned. As her mind veered off on far more interesting things he could be doing with his hands, she tried to keep her brain in the conversation. What were they talking about?

"It's better when Kennedy is around. And she'll be more help when she gets back, now that the wedding is over."

"I've said I can help while she's gone."

That he'd offer so readily—again—caused a little flutter under her breast. But that didn't make it right. He'd left that life because he didn't like it. "Flynn, you're—"

Before she could get out that he was a guest, he interrupted. "Kennedy would say I'm family, and family helps. Either way, we both know I'm more than just a guest."

That more was both thrilling and terrifying. She'd wanted romance—a grand passion to file away for cold, lonely nights down the line—and Flynn was giving that to her in spades. But he also gave her friendship and far more understanding than she'd expected. It was the sort of behavior that tempted her to count on him, and Pru knew that way lay heartache. She was still searching for the right words to turn down his kind offer when Ari came in.

"I'm starved! What's for dinner?"

Pru consciously relaxed the shoulders that had gone tense beneath Flynn's hands. They weren't doing anything wrong. "I haven't fig-ured that out just yet."

"Do we have time for a game before?"

"Depends on the game, I guess. I'll be mostly tied up with slicing, dicing, and chopping, probably."

"Flynn can play with me."

It was the sort of request she'd make of Xan-der. But Flynn wasn't the indulgent big broth-er/uncle figure, who'd be around for a long-term relationship, and no doubt, board games with a middle schooler were not what he wanted to do with his limited time here. But how to get that across to Ari without making her feel like a nuisance?

"Sure, and I'd be happy to do that." He said it with the same casual ease he'd offered to dive in and work.

Pru's heart gave another dangerous flutter.

With one last squeeze of her shoulders, Flynn dropped his hands and moved toward the kitchen table. "What would you like to play?"

Ari grinned. "I'm gonna introduce you to *Redneck Life*."

Pru stifled a laugh at the utterly confused expression on Flynn's face. Oh, this would be good.

As Ari scampered toward the family room to grab the game, Pru whispered, "Thank you."

He just smiled at her.

"Do you have any nieces or nephews or cousins?" She realized she knew nothing about his family, which felt odd considering the other intimacies they'd shared.

"I'm Irish. I've got armies of cousins. A couple of nephews from my sister. Murphy— he'd be the eldest—is nearly ten."

"Is it just the one sister?" Pru asked, tugging open the freezer to check their options.

"Just the one. She's a few years older than me and terrifyingly capable of everything."

"Sounds like Maggie," Ari said, coming back in with the box.

"I'd have said like Pru, too," Flynn said.

"Oh, Pru's totally capable, but she's not scary with it."

"Standing right here, y'all." Finding a bag of shrimp, Pru decided on scampi and began hunting up the rest of the ingredients.

"It's true, though. You're all subtle and stuff," Ari insisted.

"And brilliant with it," Flynn added.

Pru wasn't comfortable with the compliment. "I'd say that's far more out of necessity than inclination."

"Heroes always rise to the occasion." With that pronouncement, Ari unfolded the game board and began to explain how to play. "It's just like the original game of Life, except it's the person who has the most teeth left who wins."

"Teeth, is it? Sounds violent."

Ari just grinned and continued spelling out the rules.

Heroes. Pru didn't feel like anybody's hero. She was just doing everything she could to keep her family together. Watching the two of them, heads bent toward each other at the kitchen table, it was far too easy to let the fantasy expand to include him here, like this. Part of a family. Which so wasn't happening. That wasn't part of their agreement, wasn't what he was here for. Better to banish that thought for good before she started expecting things. She was in this for the now, not the future. She'd do well to remember that.

"MY TWO O'CLOCK IS GETTING SETTLED," Pru said. "The answering machine is on in case anybody calls looking for a reservation. The two girls from Memphis are still out hiking. There's a couple coming in from Milwaukee and a student from Nashville coming in for the weekend, but none of them are due until after four. Their rooms are already prepped, and I'll be out before they get here, so you shouldn't have to do anything while I'm tied up."

Flynn set his guitar aside and crossed to her, skimming his hands from her shoulders down to take her hands in his. "I'll be fine. I told you I'm here to help. It'd be nice if you'd let me."

He'd learned long ago that getting a strong woman to accept help was often an uphill battle. They were so accustomed to doing everything for themselves that they usually had it all done before anybody else could lift a finger. It had taken him and Ari both to wrestle dish duty away from her the last couple of nights. Five days post-wedding and Flynn was still watching, looking for where he could do more to relieve her stress than taking her to bed. Not that he wasn't enjoying every moment they could snatch for that noble pursuit, but he wanted to give her the break she deserved.

"I just want you to enjoy your time here and not feel like you're working."

"*Mo mhuirnín*, I'm enjoying myself just fine, and I wouldn't have offered if I didn't mean it."

Her cheeks pinked. "Well, I'm glad to hear it."

Not bothering to repress his grin, Flynn lifted both her hands to his lips for a quick kiss.

"Will it disturb anyone if I take my guitar out on the porch? I've a mind to do some writing."

"Not from the front, it won't. Go ahead." She jerked a thumb in the general direction of the treatment room. "I should…"

God, she was cute when she was flustered.

"I'll see you when you're done."

Still grinning to himself, Flynn carried his guitar and a notebook out to the front of the house. He lowered down to the top step, leaning against one of the porch posts and letting the scrap of melody that had been turning over and over in his head since his arrival begin to unfurl. His fingers stroked over the strings, coaxing the slow, faintly melancholy notes. His hero—for the song would tell a story, whether he added lyrics or not—was rolling along his path, embracing the known, the familiar, the norm. Comfortable, but with a niggle that something was missing. Until he came across something unexpected. A woman. It was always a woman. The notes shifted to warm and sweet, curious. A delightful surprise.

The song, then, would be a tale of what came after.

"Whatcha working on?"

"I'm writing a song." Flynn continued to strum absently, as he shifted his attention to Ari. "Kennedy tells me you're quite the musician." He'd not had opportunity to hear her play yet, but the term prodigy had been bandied about with regularity.

Ari jerked her thin shoulders in a shrug as she sank down on the step opposite him. "I like piano."

"I can tinker enough on a piano to get by, but it's mostly strings for me—fiddle and guitar. And occasionally drums. Harmonica if nothing else is available."

"I wouldn't have pegged you for a drummer." She angled her head, as if she were trying to picture it.

"Not that kind of drums. The *bodhran*. It's a traditional Irish instrument. You usually play it with your hands."

"Sounds like you play a little bit of everything."

"To be sure. But fiddle's my first and last love for instruments."

"Did Kennedy really tour with you?"

Flynn smiled, remembering. "She really did. The voice of an angel, has Kennedy. Those were some of the best months of my life." And had led to one of his greatest friendships. Just what would Kennedy say if she knew he was sleeping with her sister? Nothing good, he could imagine.

"Why did she stop? Seems like it would be a lot of fun."

"It was. Is, for me. But a life on the road wasn't for her in the long-term. She always had her eye on coming back here, whether she'd admit it or not."

"She said you're a modern gypsy."

It was a term he'd applied to himself often enough over the years, but somehow it didn't sit quite so easily as it had before. He didn't feel so free-wheeling and unfettered as he once had.

And that was ridiculous. What was he if not what he'd always been? "I suppose I am. I've seen much of the world through my music, and that's a grand thing."

Ari tipped her head in concession of the point. "But don't you get tired of it? Being on the road all the time? Not really having a home?"

There were a dozen flippant responses he could have made, but he answered honestly. "I never tire of it exactly. But I'm always looking for something." Like the hero in his melody.

"What?"

"I don't know. I haven't found it yet." Even as he said it, a part of him was back in bed with Pru, in the quiet moments after loving her. The world over, he'd never felt anything like the comfort he felt with her in his arms. But that wasn't a thing he was about to share with her teenaged daughter. Shaking the thought away, he grinned. "Either way, I do come to roost from time to time, to write."

"You're roosting here."

Ignoring the seriousness of her expression, he nodded, "I am. And it's a grand place to do it."

"Will you stay a while longer, after Kennedy gets back?"

"I expect so. I came all this way to see her. Seems a shame to leave without getting to spend some more time with her. Besides, I need a rematch in *Redneck Life*." Ari had trounced him. By the end of the game, he'd been left with two teeth and more debt than should have been possible. Not to mention the sixteen red-headed stepchildren, all named Daryl.

She snorted with laugher. "Oh, I definitely want the chance to hear you try the hog calling contest again."

"Who knew Pru would be the hands-down winner of that one?" She'd claimed to be doing an impression of the most obnoxious Arkansas Razorbacks fan she'd ever heard. Flynn couldn't quite fathom what that would sound like in a stadium with thousands of people.

"Pru is awesome."

"She is," he agreed.

"You like her." Ari posed it as a statement, not a question.

Flynn couldn't tell if there was accusation or disapproval in her tone, but there was no sense in denying what the girl had eyes in her head to see. "I do."

"It's not like how you feel about Kennedy."

Oh boy. This kid was too astute for her own good. What was he supposed to say? For all intents and purposes, Pru was her mother. In the end, he went with the truth. "No, not like Kennedy."

Before he could figure out whether he ought to pursue the issue to suss out if Ari had a problem with that, a car pulled into the drive.

"Anybody you know?" Flynn asked.

"Nope. Maybe it's one of the new reservations."

"If it is, they're early."

The sedan rolled to a stop in front of the steps and the driver, a middle-aged man with graying sideburns and a neat goatee, stepped out, followed by a woman Flynn assumed was his wife.

"Good day to you," Flynn called. "Welcome to the Misfit Inn."

"Oh honey, he's Irish!" the woman exclaimed.

"So I can hear."

Flynn broadened his smile. "Would you be the couple from Milwaukee, then?"

"What?" For a moment, the gentleman looked baffled. "Oh, no. But we are here looking to book a room. A woman at the diner in town recommended the place. Do you have any vacancies?"

"Sure, and I think we can manage that. For how many nights?"

"Through Sunday, if possible."

Flynn knew without looking there was space. But were the other rooms all ready? "Check in's not normally until after three, but come on inside. You'll rest a bit, while we get things sorted. If you'll just take your car around the corner to the lot there."

"Excellent!"

As soon as the man and his companion slid back into their car, Flynn turned to Ari. "Where can we put them? Are the other rooms ready?"

"Beds are made. I just need to run towels up and set out the toiletries. I'll check the book."

"What information do we need from them?"

"Copy of driver's license and a credit card number. But I don't know how to run the payment program," Ari admitted.

"We'll figure it out. Run up and pick a room, while I get them settled in the lounge with… something to eat."

She scampered off, and Flynn tried to remember what he'd seen in the cupboards for snacks. As soon as the couple came up the stairs, he ushered them inside and straight to the guest lounge. "I'm Flynn Bohannon. And you'd be?"

"I'm Kenneth Talbot. And this is my wife, Michelle."

"And where would you be from, then?"

"Los Angeles."

Flynn gestured for them to take a seat. "That's grand. One of Pru's sisters lives out that way. Would you be here for business or pleasure?"

"A little of both. Mostly pleasure," Kenneth explained.

"Sure, and we can help with that. Can I offer you some coffee? Tea?"

"Coffee would be lovely," Michelle said.

"Sort yourselves out there. I'll be back in the shake of a lamb's tail."

Flynn hurried to the kitchen to start the coffee. When he opened the freezer for the beans, he spied the rolls of frozen cookie dough, neatly labeled with baking instructions. *God love the woman.* He pulled out a roll of chocolate chip, switched on the oven to the requisite temperature, and unearthed a baking sheet. Thinking freshly baked cookies would be good for the other guests, whenever they arrived, he went ahead and sliced an entire roll and popped them into the oven, before getting started on the coffee. He was searching out mugs and plates to make up a tray, when Ari came trotting down the back stairs.

"Oh, cookies. Great idea."

"Is the room all set?"

"I'm sticking them in the Dogwood Room. I checked the book. Nobody's in there this week."

"Wonderful. Do you want to take them a clipboard with the registration paperwork, while I finish this up?"

"On it!"

By the time he carried the tray in with a plateful of warm, gooey cookies, Ari was chatting cheerfully with the couple.

"Mr. Talbot works in *Hollywood!*" she declared.

"That's brilliant. Are you researching a film, then?"

"Doing some prospective location scouting," Kenneth said.

"Are those fresh cookies?" Michelle asked.

"They are, indeed. Please, help yourself."

They were still chatting half an hour later,

when Pru stepped into the room. "What's all this?"

Flynn made introductions. "They're all the way from California, here through the weekend."

"We put them in the Dogwood Room," Ari added.

"Your husband and daughter have been plying us with cookies and coffee," Michelle added. "You have such a lovely place here."

Husband and daughter. Shock rippled through Flynn, along with some sweeter emotion as he looked from Ari to Pru. He supposed they did look like a family. It made for a far more appealing idea than he'd have imagined.

Pru seemed to likewise be struggling for what to say. Ari, however, seemed to have no problem leaping into the fray. "It's a pretty awesome place to grow up. Did you always live in Los Angeles?"

"Will you excuse us for a moment?" Pru asked.

Flynn rose as she angled her head toward the hall. They continued on into the office.

"Husband?" she asked.

He lifted his hands in truce. "I didn't say a word. They assumed."

Pru seemed more flummoxed than angry about it. "Would it be weird to correct them now?"

"Probably. What does it matter? They're only here for a few days. They don't live here." And why the hell was he reluctant for her to make that correction? He wasn't husband material.

"I suppose not. I should get their details for the reservation."

"Already gotten. The paperwork's there on the desk. You just need to run the credit card. The room's ready."

"Why didn't you come get me?"

"Why should we interrupt someone's massage for a walk-in, when Ari and I could handle it?"

Pru gave him a long look before studying

the paperwork, to make sure everything was in order. Then she set it aside and wrapped her arms around him. "Thank you."

Flynn pulled her in tight and pressed a kiss to her brow. "I told you, I want to help."

"So you did." She looked again at the reservation paperwork. "I guess I'm going to let you."

CHAPTER 6

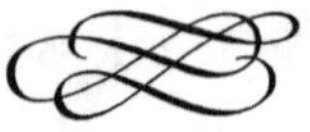

"So, FLYNN SEEMS TO be pretty settled in," Abbey observed.

Pru used the excuse of digging in the china cabinet for platters to hide her face. "I suppose a gypsy learns to settle quickly wherever he goes."

"Must be nice having that in the house."

"That?"

"A guy who looks like that. I mean, damn. You can't tell me you haven't noticed he's hot."

"A woman would have to be dead and six months buried not to notice that," Pru conceded. She passed platters to Abbey and straightened, heading for the fridge.

"He's certainly got an eye for you. He watches you whenever you're in the room."

Pru made a noncommittal noise and grabbed some bacon. What was she supposed to say to that?

"The air seems to crackle whenever you're within ten feet of each other."

"Crackle? Really?" Pru kept her voice dismissive as she began to peel some pears for an appetizer.

Abbey clutched a platter to her chest. "Oh, come *on*, Pru. Admit it! There's something going on between you and the Irish hottie."

She'd admit no such thing because the last thing she needed was something about that getting back to Kennedy. "There's attraction, yes." Pointless to deny that. "But Flynn will be leaving soon. What sense would it make to get involved with him?"

"Oh honey, being with a man like him

would have nothing to do with sense. He's the kind to make you lose your senses."

He certainly was.

"Doesn't make it any less worth it."

Pru hoped she was right.

The front door opened. A moment later, the sound of Logan's voice echoed from the foyer. "Pru?"

"In the kitchen!" she called.

He came straight back, his arms loaded down with two stacked cardboard boxes. With one look at the trays and platters scattered over the counter, he set the boxes to the side. "What's the party for and why wasn't I invited?"

"It was kind of a last-minute thing. Flynn met Ford McIntosh at the wedding and found out he was a fellow musician. Since he decided to stick around until Kennedy gets back, he invited Ford over for a jam session, and apparently Ford called every musician in the county. They're all out back." Even as she spoke, the tones of conversation and laughter gave way to more music as somebody began picking on a banjo. "Abbey, you want to go ahead and take those extra drinks to put in the cooler?"

With a look that said their discussion about Flynn wasn't over, she grabbed up the bags of drinks. "On it!"

Logan strode over to the back door as Abbey slipped out and looked at the gathering. "Holy shit. There must be near to twenty people out there."

"Twenty-two. Hence all the food." Pru slid a tray of bacon wrapped pears into the oven and moved to the boxes containing this week's farm share from Logan's CSA program. "What have we got this week?"

"Some fresh broccoli, carrots, and sugar snap peas, if you wanna put together a veggie tray. Assorted greens, tomatoes, peppers. A couple of onions. Zucchini, of course."

She mentally reviewed the other ingredients she had on hand and figured she could put out crudités with an herbed cream cheese—Athena had left an easy recipe—and maybe make some quick blender salsa to go with the bags of tortilla chips from the pantry. She grabbed what she wanted and took it to the sink to rinse. "Thanks so much for bringing this by this week. Things have been so crazy trying to juggle my clients and the inn with Kennedy being gone, I just couldn't get down to the farm."

"Not a problem. Everything going okay? Need me to pitch in with anything?" She loved that he'd offer.

"No, thanks. This was great. We're managing." Largely because of Flynn, but she didn't see the need in saying that.

"Have you heard from the newlyweds?"

"Not a word, which is as it should be. They deserve a chance to be cocooned in their own little world." And it meant she avoided any awkward questions about Flynn.

"So, Flynn's still around." It wasn't a question but Pru was determined not to feel awkward.

"He is." She scrubbed up the fresh carrots. "He's been helping out, while Kennedy is away."

"Helping out, huh?" He went quiet, his face

set in what she imagined he thought of as non-judgment.

Pru just sliced the tops off the carrots. "Your therapist tricks won't work on me, Logan. I have nothing to confess."

"Who said anything about confession? Not me."

Realizing he'd picked up on something, Pru said the only thing she could think of to turn the conversation. "No, I don't suppose you do want to confess about what you got up to at the wedding."

He played dumb. "And what would that be?"

"Two words. Opal. Springs."

She glanced up in time to see his ears turning pink.

"How did you…?"

"Did you think nobody would notice the wet hair when you got back?" Pru took some pleasure in seeing the unflappable Logan Maxwell off his game. "Look, I don't know what's going on with you and Athena, but I'm staying out of it."

He looked toward the door, where a blistering fiddle joined the fray. "Message received."

"What message?"

"You stay out of my stuff, and I stay out of yours."

It wasn't what she'd been saying, but if that was his takeaway, fine. She didn't want to answer questions right now.

"You're welcome to stay for snacks and music."

"Actually, I was thinking I'd see if Ari wanted to go riding tomorrow. If you didn't have other plans for her."

Pru softened. "She'd *love* that."

"How bout I help you finish that veggie tray and carry it out and ask her."

"Sure. Thanks." She set him up with the rest of the veggies and another platter to arrange them on, while she whipped up the dip and salsa.

Together, they carried the thrown-together feast out to the long table set up beneath the old bodock tree. All the picnic tables and most of the chairs had been arranged in a horseshoe around it, and musicians sat on every surface. Strings were well-represented, with multiple guitars, three banjos, two mandolins, a couple of other fiddles, in addition to Flynn's, and even a stand-up bass. There were also a couple of harmonicas and even a dulcimer. The Talbots and the Simpkins—the sweet, older couple from Milwaukee—were camped out in loungers from the porch, grinning broadly as the group finished up a rousing rendition of "Rocky Top".

"Wonderful!" Joanne Simpkins applauded with enthusiasm. "Oh, this is such fun. Do you always have live music?"

"We're trying something new," Pru told her.

"You ought to make this a regular thing," Kenneth Talbot said. "This would be quite the draw."

"We'll give it some thought," Pru promised. She supposed the other musicians might be talked into coming for a jam session with each other, even if Flynn wasn't around anymore. But she didn't know if she wanted the reminder. "We've got some light appetizers to tide you over. Please, enjoy!"

A few people set their instruments aside and came to fill a plate.

Done with her work for a bit, Pru perched on the edge of one of the picnic tables to enjoy the music.

"Ari and I have one to share that's a bit more from my part of the world." Flynn looked to Ari. "Are you ready, *cailín beag*?"

She nodded, and Pru watched in fascination as Flynn drew his bow across the strings and Ari began to sing. *"There were three old gypsies came to our hall door..."*

On the second verse, some of the guitarists picked up the tune, adding rhythm beneath her sweet, sassy voice. Pru hadn't even known she could sing. When had she learned this?

"Then saddle for me my milk white steed, my big horse is not speedy-oh." Flynn's voice rose, as

smooth and dynamic as his fiddle. The sound gave Pru chills.

They sparked off each other, hamming it up as they alternated verses, clearly having an absolute ball. Pru was torn between bursting with pride and wanting to burst into joyful tears. Her girl was *performing.* When the song was over, she stood up, clapping and whistling with all the others.

Joanne Simpkins leaned over. "You have a lovely family."

The smile and, "Thanks," were automatic. It wasn't until she caught Logan's raised brow that the implications sank in. With them came both pleasure and pain, because she could see it, too. How the three of them looked as a family. They'd slipped into it so easily, and the seduction of that picture was greater than all of Flynn's skill in bed. But it was an illusion. A temporary state of affairs that would be over before she could blink. Pru knew, then, that she wasn't walking away from this affair unscathed. Despite her best intentions, she was falling for

Flynn, and she didn't think she could stop herself.

⌐⌐

FLYNN ADMIRED the smooth expanse of Pru's bare back as she plucked her shirt—or what was left of it—off the lampshade. "I'll buy you a new shirt."

She bent to pick up the scraps of her panties. "Mmhmm. And these?"

"What if I prefer you without them?"

Her arch look was entirely ruined by the color that leapt into her cheeks. "Well, as I can't very well wear any of this downstairs, you're donating a shirt to the cause." She bent to grab one out of the drawer. One he'd found neatly folded and put away earlier in the week because she'd tossed his laundry in with theirs. The shirt dwarfed her, hanging down to mid-thigh. She wasn't the first woman he'd ever seen in one of his shirts, but she was the only one who'd made him salivate and stir at the sight.

Pru pointed a finger at him. "No."

Grinning, Flynn rolled off the bed, still naked, and stalked her across the room. She feinted left, dodged right and tried to get to the door, but he caught her around the waist and tumbled her back onto his bed. Her laughter bubbled up like champagne and made him feel about as intoxicated. This woman…

He trailed kisses across her cheeks, down her throat, pressing his face into the V of the shirt as his hands snaked beneath the hem.

Pru swatted at him. "You can't possibly."

"Not for a bit yet, but you can." With erotic intent, he set out to prove it.

"Flynn Bohannon, you're going to kill me. Stop. Seriously."

His hand stilled on her thigh.

"Much as I appreciate being well and truly ravished—"

"Three times," he said, smugly.

"—we don't have time for this. Ari will be home from Logan's soon, and there's no telling when the Talbots will be back from Gatlinburg or when the Simpkins come in from their afternoon hike. I need to shower, so I don't smell like sex. And we need to change your sheets."

"How about I join you in the shower and we deal with the sheets after?"

"If you join me in the shower, that will lead to shower sex, and, as appealing a thought as that may be, we don't have time for *that* either." She wriggled away from him and began to gather her clothes.

Accepting that their afternoon tryst was over—for now anyway—Flynn rolled off the bed and tugged on his jeans. "Fine. I'll strip the sheets and come down with you to start laundry." Maybe he could talk his way into her shower from there.

As he'd expected, she stayed to help him strip the bed. He gathered the linens together in a wad and nodded toward the door. "After you."

"You should put on a shirt."

"I'll get one when I come back up." To solve the issue, he scooted by her and headed for the stairs.

By the second-floor landing, Flynn's stomach was making itself heard. "If I can't talk you back into bed, can I at least talk you into a snack?"

"Well, we certainly worked up an appetite. I'll see what I can—"

Flynn stopped dead halfway down the stairs, so fast that Pru ran into his back.

A woman stood in the foyer. Not one of the guests. She wore a skirt and blouse, with shoes that said sensible rather than Saturday. A briefcase hung from one shoulder, and the expression on her face made it obvious she'd overheard their conversation and knew exactly how they'd been spending their afternoon.

Shite.

"Pru Reynolds?" Even the woman's voice sounded pinched. It was nasal and full of disdain.

Pru tucked in closer to his back, using him to shield her pantsless state. "Yes. May I help you?"

Flynn had to give it to her—despite the

compromising position they found themselves in, her tone was as smooth and friendly as it would be for any guest.

"I'm Lydia Coogan, with the Department of Human Services. I'm the new social worker assigned to Ari Rosas."

"New social worker?" Pru's voice went sharp with concern. "What happened to Mae?"

"Miss Bradley is out on extended medical leave."

"Is she okay?"

"I believe she's having some kind of surgery." Clearly, she didn't really know her predecessor and didn't care. Lydia's gaze shifted from Pru to Flynn. "And you would be?"

This woman controlled Ari's fate. He couldn't imagine how bad it looked for Pru to be caught sleeping with a guest, so he said the only thing he could think of. "Flynn Bohannon. Pru's fiancé."

Pru's fingers dug into his back—because of his words or because, at that moment, the front door opened, Flynn wasn't sure. The newcomers came in on the tail end of the statement.

Ari gave a whoop. "You finally asked her! Yay!"

What the hell?

Logan's mouth dropped open as he shut the door. "Man, what's in the water around here? First Kennedy and now Pru."

"I—" Pru finally moved around him on the stairs, looking like she was about to keel over. "Excuse me for just a few minutes." She disappeared back toward her bedroom, presumably to get dressed. Realizing he still held the wad of sheets, Flynn excused himself as well, high tailing it to the laundry room and dumping them in the washer. He grabbed a t-shirt from the hamper and tugged it on, before hurrying back to do damage control.

Lydia was giving Logan the side eye now. "And who are you?"

"Family friend," he said easily.

Pru came back, dressed in her own clothes, her hair brushed and pulled back into a tail.

Whatever color their afternoon of lovemaking had whipped into her cheeks was gone. "Logan, thanks for bringing Ari home."

"No problem." He shot her a look that might have been an apology for the timing.

"If you could keep the news under your hat, I would appreciate it."

"I can do that. Congratulations."

She opened her mouth as if to say thank you, then closed it again without a word. Instead, she just nodded.

Logan shot a look at the social worker. "You need anything, just let me know."

"Thanks."

Once he was gone, Pru turned to Lydia. "Can we start over? Would you come into the living room?"

The woman looked as if she wanted to refuse, but she followed.

Ari caught Flynn's eye and gave him a double thumbs up. Jesus, what had he set in motion?

"I don't think we need you for this just now,"

he said. No doubt Pru was about to set the social worker straight. They could explain to Ari later. "Why don't you go wash up for supper? You smell like horse."

"'K." She ran up the stairs.

Flynn hurried into the living room, joining Pru on the sofa and taking her hand in his. He expected her to jerk it away and explain to the woman that it was all a lie. Instead, she curled her fingers around his. He could feel her shaking.

"Miss Coogan, I apologize for our introduction. I assure you, that's not…usual." Flynn thought for a moment she'd go on. But, really, what else was there to say?

Lydia took out a notepad. "Well, this changes things."

Pru's cheeks went impossibly paler. "What do you mean?"

"There's nothing about Mr. Bohannon in my case records. If he's going to be a part of the household, he'll have to go through the same approval process you did before we can do the home study."

"But that's months more waiting!"

Flynn had no idea what she'd already gone through to get approved thus far, but this sounded very much like starting over. A sick feeling set up in his gut. "Is there nothing else to be done? She's already come this far."

"Well, you can apply for an exception." The admission came grudgingly. "It's still sixty days, but it's quicker than all the other certification processes."

"Then we'll do that," Flynn said.

"And if the exception isn't approved?" Pru asked.

"Then we find Ari a new placement." Lydia's lips pursed with disapproval. "She shouldn't have been in the home in the first place without all these certifications complete, but Mae seems to be rather lax about such things."

"She was friends with my mother for twenty-five years. And my mother took in more foster children than any other single person in all of Stone County."

"Rules exist for a reason," Lydia insisted. "But we're working with the situation we have. You'll need to go down to the Department of Human Services to pick up the paperwork to file the exception to policy."

"And once that's done?" Pru asked.

"Get the exception filed. I'll be in touch about the rest." With a few more notations on her pad, she shoved it into her briefcase. "I'll see myself out."

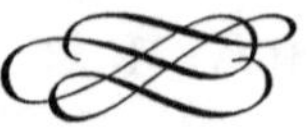

SHOCK KEPT PRU IMMOBILE as Lydia Coogan left the room. There was probably something she should have said, but she had no idea what. There was no proper protocol for this situation, no Emily Post guide to the right way to handle being caught with your lover by your foster child's social worker. The only possible way it could have been worse would have been if she'd walked in on them *in flagrante*. Even that could have been explained. Maybe. It wasn't as if celibacy was a mandatory requirement for fostering and adoption. But this?

As the front door shut, Pru found the strength to pull away and round on Flynn. "What the hell were you *thinking? Engaged?*"

He ran a hand through his hair—still mussed from her fingers. Jesus. And Ari had seen her standing in his shirt.

"I panicked. I was trying to protect your reputation—sleeping with your fiancé certainly seemed better than sleeping with a guest."

His panic response was to invent a proposal? Pru shoved up from the couch to pace. "Okay, *maybe*, under any other circumstance that would make some measure of sense. But that woman controls whether the adoption goes through. You heard her. By making this announcement, you're now a part of this. And what's it going to look like when my brand-new fiancé up and hits the road in a couple of weeks? This is a disaster! I'm going to lose her." Fear rose up and gripped her by the throat. "Oh

God, I'm going to lose her, all because I was foolish enough to think I could have something for myself."

Pru covered her mouth to hold back the sob. What had she done? She'd made Ari a promise, and because of her selfish desire to do something else, be something more, she'd jeopardized that promise and the family the girl had come to trust.

Flynn crossed to her in two strides, wrapping strong arms around her. "You won't lose Ari. You won't. It will be all right, *mo mhuirnín.*"

"How?" she demanded, wanting to shove away, yet needing the support. How the hell had she come to depend on him so fast?

"I'll stay." The simple words fell between them with all the gravity of stone, sure and solid as a foundation, and so much what she wanted she could hardly breathe. "I'll fill out the paperwork, submit to the background check, do whatever's necessary to make this happen."

Pru could only stare at him, looking into the blue eyes so steady on hers. She didn't dare believe what she was hearing. "You're seriously willing to stick around for possibly months, faking an engagement to me, to make this work? Because that's what this will be. Months. In one place. You haven't stayed put that long anywhere since you were eighteen."

If he felt an iota of panic over the idea of it, he didn't show it. Instead, he framed her face in gentle hands. "I got you into this mess. I'll get you out. I won't let your involvement with me damage what you've built for that child."

The heart that had been opening to him from the moment they'd met simply rolled over and exposed its tender underbelly. That he'd be willing to do this—change his whole life, whatever plans he'd made for the next several months—for her, for Ari—simply undid her. Still, good intentions aside, she had to make him see what he was really getting into.

"Think about what you're saying, Flynn. We

have to convince *everyone* that we're really engaged."

"That's not exactly a hardship, Pru. I like you. I respect you. And God knows, I'm attracted to you. Hell, the guests already think we're married."

A fact which had given her pause more than once, but she hadn't seen the point in correcting people who wouldn't be around longer than a few days. "The guests aren't who she'll be interviewing. This whole process means your life gets put under a microscope. She'll be talking with your friends, your family, and all of mine. How are we going to explain this? None of those people knows we're involved. None of them can shed light on our history together because we don't have one. And it doesn't look any better to be engaged to a man I've known two weeks."

"We create a backstory." He pulled her back to the sofa to sit, keeping her hands in his. "You came to Ireland to visit Kennedy two years ago. We met then and have been carrying on a long-distance relationship ever since."

She frowned at him. "You thought of that awfully fast."

He stroked a finger along her cheek. "I was thinking it was a shame we didn't meet when you came over on that trip. And that a week or two wouldn't have been enough. I still don't think it's enough. So, yes, I'll do this. I'll stay."

Pru wanted so desperately to believe him. He meant it—or thought he did, at least. But how long would that last? How long before he grew to resent her and the situation she'd inadvertently trapped him in? Faced with the alternative of losing Ari, she was too terrified not to go through with this lunatic scheme. But she couldn't help but feel that the end result of the whole thing would be either disaster or heartbreak or both.

"Then I guess we have a lot of details to figure out."

"We'll get through this," he promised.

She could only pray that he was right.

"What will you tell your sisters?"

At the thought of having to tell them any-thing—truth or lie—Pru wanted to curl up into a ball. "I have no idea. Kennedy will know the backstory is bullshit, as I was with her the whole time on that trip. Maggie will disapprove of this whole thing, whether she gets the truth or the lie. And Athena is the loose cannon."

"We've got most of a week to figure out what to say to Kennedy."

"We'll need some story in place before then. Logan will probably keep quiet because I asked him to, but I don't know who this Coogan woman may know locally. Once anybody catches wind of it, the whole town will know by nightfall. We've got to be ready to answer questions when they come."

"And we will be."

As the whole thing rolled through her mind again, Pru zeroed in on a detail she hadn't processed at the time. "Why did my child say that you'd 'finally' asked me? What have you been saying to her?"

"Nothing. She knows I like you and that it's definitely not the sister or friend vibe I feel for Kennedy. It seemed pointless to deny the truth when she brought it up. But I swear the conversation didn't go any further."

Pru didn't know if that made her feel better or worse. But it highlighted another prospective pitfall of this plan. "Ari has a sweet, romantic heart. She was highly entertained by Kennedy and Xander getting back together, and with their wedding and all, I'm sure she's imagining everybody paired off with somebody. She likes you. She lights up around you."

"Likewise. She's a great kid." He meant it. She'd seen the genuine pleasure he took in hanging out with her.

"She is. But if we do this, I think we have to tell her the truth. The alternative is her getting comfortable with the idea of you being around permanently, of you being her father. She's had far too much disappointment and lost far too many people she cared about to put her through that again when you go." Pru closed her eyes. "I can't believe I'm about to ask her to lie about this."

Mom of the year, here I come.

"I'm on board with the plan." Ari popped in from the hallway.

Pru just sighed. Of course, she'd probably heard everything. "What did we say about eavesdropping?"

"I couldn't just bust up in the middle of all that. You needed to finish that conversation."

Pru opened her mouth, closed it again. No sense in chastising her right now. Better to talk directly about the situation they found themselves in. "Do you understand what's going on?"

"New social worker disapproves of you having an adult relationship, so Flynn tried to cover, and it's easier to go with it than try to explain the lie."

Flynn made a sort of choking cough that might have been comical under other circumstances. "That's a remarkably succinct description."

Ari flopped into a chair, draping her legs

over the arm. "Really, it feels a bit like living in a soap opera."

"This is a lot more serious than a soap opera," Pru said. "I'd never agree to something like this under normal circumstances. But these aren't normal circumstances. That woman can take you away from me if she deems me unfit."

"Not gonna happen," Flynn insisted. "You're an amazing mother, and it won't take her long to figure that out."

Ari pointed at him. "And that is why everybody will believe he's the real deal. Also, he's not wrong. You're an awesome mom. You being human doesn't change that."

Emotion welled in the back of Pru's throat. "I appreciate the vote of confidence."

Ari swung around in the chair, propping her elbows on her knees and her chin in her hands. "Now, tell me the proposal story. You'll need a good one."

"You *do* have a romantic streak," Flynn observed.

Ari just grinned. "Takes one to know one, boy-o."

GIVEN the mobile nature of Flynn's lifestyle, he hadn't attended church services with any particular regularity since he'd left home. It had been more of the occasional yen than a priority. But Sunday morning found him settling into a pew of the First United Methodist Church of Eden's Ridge. Pru sat beside him, with Ari on her other side. They garnered a few curious looks from other attendees. No doubt, they were wondering who exactly he was. Flynn offered up a polite smile and nod as he took Pru's hand in his and turned his attention to Reverend Hodgson, who'd officiated Kennedy and Xander's wedding.

"The grace of the Lord Jesus Christ be with you."

The congregation replied, "And also with you."

As the service rolled on, Flynn stood when the others stood, sang when the others sang, sat when they sat. But the content barely registered. He was too busy mulling over the situation they were in. Thinking about the implications of what he'd agreed to. He was the one who'd started this, and now the three of them were caught up in a monumental lie. He was grateful this wasn't a Catholic church because he was feeling the need to confess. How many Hail Marys and Our Fathers would it take to make up for this? More, probably, than he could say in a lifetime. Father Doyle, the priest from his childhood parish, would skin him alive. But Flynn had made Pru a promise, and he intended to keep it.

Exhaustion dragged at him. He and Pru had been up half the night going through an intensive Get To Know You session, filling in the gaps and small details in their knowledge of each other. The more he learned, the more fascinated he became. She had so much heart, and it floored him how much she gave of herself.

Family came first for her, always. Except for the decision to get involved with him.

And look where that got her.

She was trusting him. Trusting that he'd follow through on the promise he'd made. But Flynn knew, deep down, she didn't really believe he'd stay. She'd had their end in mind from the beginning. And why shouldn't she? He had nearly half a lifetime that painted him as the gypsy she believed him to be. That image had never bothered him before her. He wanted to be more for her. He wanted to be more *with* her. But a woman like that would believe actions instead of words.

Flynn looked down at the hand he held, seeing the naked ring finger. He'd do right by her. He'd do right by her and Ari both.

At the end of the service, they joined the line of people exiting the church. As they reached Reverend Hodgson, he took Flynn's hand in a warm shake. "Mr. Bohannon. I didn't expect to see you still here. Enjoying the hospitality of our little town?"

"I am." Flynn resisted the urge to look at Pru. "Actually, I wondered if you could use me for some music next Sunday."

"An offertory? That'd be splendid! You played so well at the wedding."

"I'll be in touch in a day or so about what you'd like me to play." Maybe it would count for a Hail Mary or two.

"Sounds great! And Pru, how are things at the inn with your sister off on her honeymoon?"

"Oh, they're going fine. Ari's been a great help." Pru wrapped an arm around the girl's shoulders. "Flynn, too."

"Good to hear. Good to hear."

Sensing Pru's discomfort, Flynn pressed a hand to the small of her back, and they began to edge away.

"See you next week!" Ari called.

No one spoke until they were buckled into Pru's car and driving away from the church.

"Well, no one knows anything yet or we'd have heard about it." Pru loosed a sigh. "I half expected to burst into flames as we stepped into the sanctuary."

And wasn't that a cheerful thought.

Ari leaned forward from the back seat. "You realize you're going to have to get over the anxiety of telling people, right?"

"There's too much at stake for me not to be anxious."

"So give them a reason for the anxiety," he said. "It's been a long-standing, secret relationship, and you don't think your sisters will approve."

Her gaze flicked to him. "Long-standing or not, no I don't think they will approve, so that's at least a little bit of truth to hang on to."

The truth shouldn't have stung. He'd known going into this that Kennedy would be pissed if he got involved with Pru. He'd made his peace with that. But he couldn't stand the idea that Pru regretted what was between them. This time with her had been some of the best of his life. He wouldn't change a minute of it—except for coming down those stairs. He had a feeling she might be wishing she could rewind back to the night of the wedding and run the other way. Given the risks to her family, to Ari, Flynn couldn't blame her. His only alternative was to do everything in his power to make sure she didn't regret taking a chance on him.

Back at the house, they split up to go change out of church clothes. Flynn caught Ari on the second floor. "Hey, I need your help with something."

"Sure."

He tugged her into one of the empty rooms and shut the door, keeping his voice low as he told her what he needed. Then he had to slap a hand over her mouth to keep her squeal from echoing down the stairs.

"Shhh! Do you think you can do it?"

"Well duh. I'm going with you. You know that, right?"

He grinned. "I thought you might. Go work your magic. I'll change and work on convincing her to let you off for the rest of the day."

Ari saluted. "You can count on me."

"Get your face under control or she'll ask questions."

The girl immediately pokered up.

"Nicely done, *cailín beag.*"

She slipped out into the hall like a burglar, and he repressed a laugh. That kid was too much fun.

After he'd changed, he found Pru in the kitchen. "I went ahead and stripped and changed the sheets from the Simpkins' room. Figured we could get started turning that since they checked out this morning. Bed's remade, but the room will need fresh towels and such." He carried the linens to the laundry room, added them to the partial load waiting in the washer, and started the machine.

"I was going to get to that," she said.

"And now you don't have to." He brushed his lips lightly over hers, meaning to offer just a friendly peck. But she sighed and melted into him. That instant surrender just did him in, every time. He wrapped his arms around her and slid deeper into the kiss. Not raging heat, just a quiet comfort that he found more appealing than he'd have imagined.

A throat cleared.

Flynn was surprised and pleased when Pru didn't bolt away but rested her head on his chest as she stayed in his arms.

"Might as well get used to it, kid," she said.

"I learned how to walk loudly with Kennedy and Xander. I got this."

Flynn snorted.

"You think she's kidding. She's not." Pru eased away.

"Did you ask her?" Ari demanded.

"Ask me what?"

"I was hoping you'd let me borrow Ari for the rest of the day."

"For what?"

He'd given this some thought and decided they'd add this to the trip. "She's expressed some interest in learning to play the fiddle. As I'm going to be here for a while, I want to get her one. There's a shop in Gatlinburg."

Pru's mouth dropped open. "That's incredibly generous."

Flynn hooked an arm around Ari's shoulders, surprised and pleased when she swung a companionable arm behind his back. "Talent like this should be nurtured."

"I wish I could go with you, but I need to stay here to deal with guests."

"We'll make a day of it, if you don't mind. And you can have an afternoon more or less to yourself. The Talbots were off to Blowing Rock for the day, so maybe you can relax a bit. Have a bath. Do some reading."

She gave a considering look. "I could—"

Flynn gripped her by the shoulders. "*Don't* say catch up on paperwork. Do something for yourself."

"Okay, okay. I'll come up with something that…isn't that."

He pressed a kiss to her brow. "We'll try to be back by dinner."

Once he and Ari were in the car she asked, "Did you mean it? About the fiddle?"

"If you want. I figured we could kill two birds with one stone."

"Sweet!" She pumped her fist in the air.

"Did you get it?"

Reaching into her pocket, she pulled out a ring. "She left it on the holder on the kitchen sink, when she did the breakfast dishes this morning."

"Excellent. You're a good little partner in crime."

"That's partner in romance, buddy. I'm gonna help you knock her socks off." She spent the entire two-hour drive telling him how.

The first two shops were a bust. The rings were either out of his budget, tacky, or simply wouldn't suit Pru. Even if she wasn't wearing his ring for life, he wanted to pick something she'd like.

"Maybe it was too much to hope we could knock this out in a day," he said.

"Let's just try one more place," Ari insisted. She consulted the search she'd brought up on her phone. "There's another one about half a mile that way."

Celtic flutes greeted them as they walked inside the next shop. An older woman behind the counter smiled. "Can I help you?"

"We're looking for engagement rings," Flynn said.

"They're not what we typically specialize in, but I can certainly show you what we have." She gestured them over to a display case in the back. "I'm afraid we only have these two trays."

Flynn and Ari hunkered down, peering through the glass at the offerings. These were far more to his taste, with knotwork that spoke to his heritage. There were simple silver claddaghs, with their hands clasping a crowned heart. The sentiment he approved of, but he wanted something with a bit more style.

Then he saw it at the back. It was clearly inspired by the traditional Claddagh ring, but the hands were replaced by Celtic knotwork, and a round cut diamond was nestled in a setting that mimicked the claddagh's heart and crown. Not huge—he couldn't afford huge—but beautiful. Even as he pointed, Ari lifted her hand and they both said, "That one."

Flynn listened to the sales pitch, taking in the details about the clarity and quality of the diamond. Half an hour later, they walked out with the ring in a box in his pocket.

"It's perfect," Ari declared.

He had to agree.

"Now you have to decide how to give it to her. You can't just hand it over."

Amused, he gave her a sidelong glance. "Believe it or not, I've romanced a woman or two in my time."

"Yeah, but none of them were Pru."

Well, she was right about that. As they headed back to where they'd left the car, Flynn looked down at her. "Tell me something, *cailín beag.* When you walked in on us yesterday, why did you say that I'd finally asked her?"

"I pegged that woman as a social worker in zero point three seconds, and I'd heard you announce yourself as Pru's fiancé. I figured you'd just blurted it out and could use some back up. Besides, it seemed like an inevitable conclusion."

"Did it now?" Flynn unlocked the car.

Ari tugged open her door and gave him a very adult look over the top of the car. "Please. I've seen the way you look at her."

"And how's that?"

"Like little heart-eyed cartoon birdies are circling your head. You, Mr. Irishman, are hooked." On that pronouncement, she got in and shut the door.

Flynn was afraid she was in the way of being right.

PRU FINISHED TURNING the room because then it was done and ready for the next guest. While she was up there, she did a quick tidy of the Talbots' room, making the bed, replacing the towels. Then she headed down to the little office to check messages and emails, in case there were more reservations. She decided that didn't count as paperwork but just good business. There were two email requests—one for a weekend in August, and one for a week around Labor Day. She emailed them both back, then tried to decide what to do just for her.

She had no idea. Going after Flynn was the first thing she'd done for herself in years. Well, that wasn't entirely true. She'd done small things for herself, maintaining little rituals and relaxations, when she'd lived alone. Those had mostly fallen by the wayside when she'd moved in to take care of Ari after Joan's death. Everything normal had fallen by the wayside then. She hadn't minded coming back to this house. Not really. The best memories of her life were here. It was, quite simply, home. She was comfortable here, and she prided herself on making guests feel the same. It wasn't that far off from how she'd been when welcoming new fosters into the fold. She'd been the one to comfort, to find the little things to ease their difficult transition. Recognizing and anticipating those needs was simply second nature to her now. So why couldn't she recognize and accept her own?

The sound of the front door opening drew her out of the office. The Talbots strode in. Kenneth had the phone pressed to his ear, talking a mile a minute. "No, no, you'll love it. It's perfect. Well, no there are some prospective issues with the spot…"

Michelle trailed behind him, giving a smile and an indulgent roll of her eyes when she caught sight of Pru. As he headed on up the stairs, she stayed behind.

"Y'all are back earlier than I expected. I thought you were headed to Blowing Rock today."

"We were. Then he stumbled across a prospective location somewhat nearer and wanted to call his people about it, so we're back here." Michelle dropped her voice. "Between you and me, I'm not crying about not being in the car all day. I've been enjoying relaxing here."

"Would you like a cup of tea or some coffee? I was just about to make some."

"That would be lovely."

The older woman followed Pru into the kitchen—not an area guests were usually allowed in, but as she hadn't decided what she wanted to do with herself, entertaining someone else for a bit seemed like a good plan.

"Help yourself to the cookie jar," Pru invited.

"Don't mind if I do." Michelle drew out one of the snickerdoodles from yesterday and sat on one of the barstools. "Quiet here this afternoon. Where are your husband and daughter?"

Pru put the kettle on. "Fiancé, actually. He and Ari area headed down to Gatlinburg for the afternoon."

Well, look at that. She didn't get immediately struck by lightning at the admission and didn't start hyperventilating. Did that count as progress?

"I hope you don't mind me saying, but he's

just delicious. That accent." Michelle gave a little shiver.

"He is," Pru conceded. "And yes, the accent is wonderful."

"However did you wind up with an Irishman?"

Now was her chance to try on this lie for someone who didn't actually matter. "He's best friends with one of my sisters. She lived abroad for a decade, and I went to visit her in Ireland two years ago and met Flynn."

With a dreamy expression that reminded her a little of Ari, Michelle propped her chin on one hand. "Was it love at first sight?"

"No. Lust, certainly—" That much was the absolute truth. "—But love came later. After I came home, we stayed in touch. Calls, emails, Skype. Kennedy had no idea. She just got married recently, and he was in town for that and stayed on after. One thing led to another and…engaged."

"So, you're newly engaged?"

"Very."

"Congratulations! That's so exciting. What did your sister say?"

"We haven't told her yet. She's still on her honeymoon. And we're still trying to figure out how to break it to her, when the whole relationship has been a secret. To all of my sisters, actually."

"They'll be surprised, I imagine, but surely they'll be happy for you. Anybody looking at the two of you can see you're right together."

Pru smiled a little. It certainly felt that way, and she had no doubt that feeling would only intensify, the longer he was here. And where did that leave her when it ended and he was free to go back to his gypsy ways? "He's not at all what any of them imagined for me." He was the last thing Pru had dared imagine for herself.

"Psh. It's a rare thing that our family knows what we need in a relationship. My family thought I should end up with an accountant. Stodgy, practical sort. They were perfectly scandalized when I married Kenneth. The only mollifying factor for my mother was that he wasn't an actor. You can't let your family interfere with who you love."

Pru wished it were that simple. That this was simply the course of a normal relationship and the lie about how they'd met was real. If it were merely her sisters' disapproval of that, she could cope with it. But the reality…

As the afternoon wore on, worry continued to niggle her, distracting her from the movie she tried to watch and the book she tried to read. In the end, she took a glass of wine into the bathroom and had a long, hot bubble bath, then fell into bed for a rare nap. She woke, hours later, when she heard someone moving around in the kitchen. Her family was home. Rubbing sleep from her eyes and running a quick brush through her hair, Pru went to join them.

"Oh my gosh, you have to see it! It's beautiful!" Ari exclaimed, clutching the instrument case to her chest.

Her enthusiasm made it easier to find a genuine smile. "Well, let's go into the family room and see."

Pru was aware of Flynn's eyes on her as she followed Ari. As the girl carefully laid out the case and opened it, he slid an arm around her waist, pressing a kiss to her brow in a wordless comfort that made her ache, even as it soothed.

"Isn't it gorgeous?" Ari showed her the whole set up, describing every piece, showing how it fit together, and even drawing the bow very discordantly across the strings.

Pru tried not to wince.

"We'll have proper lessons starting tomorrow," Flynn promised. "When we're sure no one is sleeping."

Ari took no offense at that. "I can't wait! Thank you, Flynn!" She threw her arms around him in a fierce hug.

"Why don't you go put it away, then have some of that pizza we brought home?"

Home. Her home. Ari's home. But could it be his home? Could he learn to love it here, as they did? Or would he reach a point where he felt trapped?

"Pru?"

She jolted. "What?"

"I asked if you'd eaten. We're later than we planned."

"I—" She glanced out the window, noticed it was coming on dark. "Good lord, what time is it?"

"Near nine."

She hadn't heard a peep from the Talbots. They must have gone into town for dinner. "No, I haven't had anything for a while. I'm not really hungry."

Flynn searched her face, and she had the sense he saw way more than she wanted him to.

"Come with me." He pulled her outside, down the steps and toward the barn.

"Why are we going to the barn?"

"For some privacy." He didn't flip on the overhead lights, instead plugging in the twinkle lights they had yet to take down. "There now, tell me what's wrong."

She considered half a dozen things to do with the inn. But that would just be a delay tactic, and she felt she owed him honesty. "I don't know if I can do this."

He didn't ask which part. Maybe he just knew. Maybe it didn't matter. But he took her hands in his. "I'm sorrier than I can say that I made things harder for you. That was never my intention. Tell me how I can make this better. Tell me what you need me to do, and I'll do it."

He'd try. And Pru loved that about him. She'd come to love so many things about him.

"I don't know. We can't hit the rewind button. There's no way to undo what Lydia Coogan saw. If it had been Mae, it would have been fine. She pulled every string possible to keep Ari with us after Mom died. But it wasn't Mae. We're just going to have to do the best we can and hope it's enough. I'm so damned afraid that it won't be enough. That she'll see through this charade."

"Is it just the encounter with the Coogan woman that you'd undo, if you could?" His voice was carefully neutral, but she recognized the tension underneath.

"I don't regret you, Flynn. I can't. You're a good, caring man or you wouldn't have volunteered yourself for this lunacy." She reached up to cup his face. "Thanks for being that guy."

He bent brushed his lips to hers. "You're worth all the crazy and more, *agra*."

She sighed, pressing her brow to his. "You know one of the worst parts of all of this?"

"What's that?"

"I hate what's at stake and I hate that you've been trapped by circumstance and your own nobility, but there's a part of me that's so pitifully relieved that you're not leaving next week." The admission cost her. But she didn't want to add to the lies any more than she had to. Between the two of them, she wanted only truth. She pulled back to look at him. "I know that's probably not what you want to hear. It's not what we agreed to. But there you have it. I've gotten…attached to you. And I don't know how to face what's coming without sliding deeper into that."

Flynn skimmed his thumb along her cheek. "Then don't fight it. I meant what I said. A couple of weeks with you isn't enough. Even if all this hadn't happened, I'd have been looking for reasons to extend my stay. And I've never wanted to do that before. You've gotten under my skin. So, we don't fight it. We let what's already been happening happen, and that's why they'll believe it."

"And after?" she whispered.

"We don't think about the after. We take each day as it comes."

One day at a time. Yeah, she could probably do that. "Okay."

"I got you something today."

"Oh, you didn't have to do that. You made Ari so happy with that fiddle."

"That was fun, and I'll enjoy teaching her. But this was actually the whole purpose of our trip."

Pru heard the faint snap and looked down

to see an open ring box in his hand. "Oh my God."

Flynn plucked the ring out and dropped to one knee. "If we're going to do this thing, we're going to do it right. So, will you wear my ring and take what comes, with me by your side, partners 'til the end?"

She didn't know when the end would be or what it might bring. But she was too far gone to give any other answer.

"Yes."

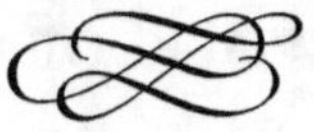

WHAT A DIFFERENCE A ring made.

Wearing Flynn's made this whole engagement feel more real. Mistake or not, it was easier to face telling people with it gracing her left hand. Pru had gotten more practice with that when they'd driven to Johnson City to pick up the exception to policy packet Monday morning, explaining her reasons for the request to the woman at DHS. Twenty minutes later, they'd left with the thick sheaf of papers and warm congratulations. They hadn't run into

Lydia Coogan, and that was a blessing. Pru had also gotten more details on Mae, who was scheduled for back surgery at the end of the week. At this stage, they weren't clear when she would be back to work or whether she would be back at all.

"Do you know if she's receiving visitors at the hospital?" Pru asked.

"Family only, right now."

Pru wondered who that would be. She knew from her mother that Mae was long divorced and had no children of her own. It was part of why they'd been friends. Mae took as much joy from helping place children as Joan had from keeping them.

Back in the car, Flynn flipped through the packet. "This is…a lot of material."

"I warned you, they'll be going through your life with a fine-toothed comb. I don't quite know how it will work since your friends and family are in Ireland, but I guarantee they'll at least call."

"Then I'd best prepare them."

She glanced his way as she navigated into traffic. "And how's that conversation gonna go?"

"Ma, Da, I met a wonderful woman, and I'm sticking around to see where it goes."

"That simple?"

He picked up her hand, kissed it. "It's the truth."

Pru wished it were just that. She wished she were the only reason he was staying. She wished she were the kind of woman who inspired that kind of devotion. "I'd say the truth is a fair bit more complicated, and they're gonna need some more details to back up our story. The whole engagement and—oh yeah—child make that a necessity."

"My mother will be so thrilled at the prospect of my settling down and acquiring another grandchild, she'll go along with anything. The hard part will be stopping her from hopping on the next plane to come welcome you both to the family."

"That sounds both awesome and terrifying."

"She can be both. She's gonna love you."

Pru didn't know what to do with the future tense. A man with one foot out the door, with an eye on the eventual end of things wouldn't talk about her meeting his mother. So what did that mean? *Don't fight it,* she reminded herself, running a thumb across the bottom of her ring. Maybe she would meet his family. Maybe in the end this would all work out.

"Where are we going now?" Flynn asked.

"The police station. Might as well get the fingerprinting over with here. I don't *think* anybody at the Sheriff's Department would call Xander on his honeymoon, but I'd just as soon not have to explain anything to them until they're actually back."

"Fair enough."

It was past time for lunch when they made it back to the inn. An unfamiliar car was parked in the lot.

"Were we expecting a reservation today?" Flynn asked.

"No. But Ari knows she was supposed to

call if anyone showed up. Maybe it's one of Abbey's clients. She was supposed to be here all morning." Except Pru didn't see Abbey's car. A trickle of unease bled through. What if this was Lydia Coogan? Pru didn't like the idea of the woman talking to Ari by herself. But surely Ari would have called if she'd shown up.

She and Flynn hurried inside, following the sound of voices back to the kitchen.

Ari sat at the kitchen table in animated conversation. She looked up and beamed as they came into the room. "Look who came back!"

"Athena? What are you doing here?"

Her youngest sister swung around, eyes narrowing in on Pru's left hand. "What. The. Literal. Fuck?"

"Language," Pru warned.

"Screw that. You're *engaged?*"

And so it begins.

Flynn pressed a hand to the small of her back and, for a moment, she leaned into his support. "I'll make the tea."

Pru took a deep breath and sat. "How did you hear?"

"Logan called me."

Damn it. Had he told anyone else? "There was no reason for him to."

"No reason? Pru, you are *engaged* to a man you barely know. No offense, Flynn."

"None taken."

"Maggie's gonna lose her shit."

Pru winced. "Did you tell her?"

"No. She's taken off enough time the past few months to come home. She can't afford to take any more, and I didn't really believe Logan when he said it. I figured there was some logical explanation for it or that he was mistaken somehow, and I could come down and sort things without needlessly upsetting her."

"Right, because it's Maggie's level of upset that's the priority here."

Athena stared at her. "Who are you and what have you done with my sister?"

Temper pricked and for once, Pru didn't try to tamp it down. "Ari, sweetheart, could you go upstairs for a bit? I need to talk to your aunt in private."

"But—"

"Now, Ari."

She screwed up her face in a snit. "Yes, ma'am."

"And actually go upstairs. No eavesdropping this time."

That added a flounce to the snit on her way out of the room. Pru would have a chat with her about that later. She waited until she heard the tromp of feet up the stairs to speak again.

"Look, I get that Maggie's stressed. We've all been stressed. But you and Maggie have both gone back to the lives you've built. I'm the one who stayed. I'm the one who's gotten no break whatsoever since Mom died. I'm the one who's changing my entire life for that child. So far be for me to actually think about myself for once."

Athena's mouth hung open. "I don't discount that you've done a lot and you totally deserve to do something for you. But for God's sake, sleep with him. There's no reason to go and marry him."

"Thanks," Flynn said dryly.

"Sorry. Just calling it like I'm seeing it."

"That was the original plan," Pru snapped. "Which was going beautifully, until Ari's new social worker arrived in time to see me in nothing but Flynn's shirt." She hadn't made a conscious decision to tell Athena the truth, but now that she'd started down that path, she'd see it through.

"*New* social worker? What happened to Mae?"

"She's out indefinitely for back surgery, and her caseload has been transferred to a hideously by-the-book woman, who'd like nothing more than to pull Ari out of this house."

"Pretending to be her fiancé seemed the lesser of available evils," Flynn said, setting mugs of tea on the table.

Pru's was doctored with half and half and a spoonful of turbinado sugar, exactly as she liked it.

Athena held up a hand. "Okay, first, good for you. I didn't imagine you had it in you. Second, let me get this straight. You're only pretending to be her fiancé to protect my sister's reputation with this social worker?"

"That's the gist of it." He lifted his own tea and sipped.

"And you don't think it looks gnarly for you to be engaged to a guy you've known two weeks?"

"Two years, according to our story. I met him when I went to visit Kennedy in Ireland, and we've had a long-distance relationship ever since."

"*Did* you meet him in Ireland?"

"No."

"So, Kennedy's gonna know this is bullshit."

"Yes."

"And you're expecting her to lie about it when asked?"

"I'm not expecting any of you to lie. As far as any of you are concerned, you didn't know anything about our relationship. That's the truth. We're the only ones lying here."

"Well, and Ari's backing us up," Flynn added.

"The kid knows?"

"More eavesdropping. It's becoming a thing," Pru said. "But I wouldn't have lied to her about this."

Athena picked up her tea. "How, exactly, is this gonna work?"

"He's got to fill out a metric ton of paperwork, go through background checks, reference checks. He got fingerprinted this morning. And it'll be sixty days before they can even think about scheduling the home visit now."

Athena shifted her attention to Flynn. "Wait, so you have to be here through all that?"

He nodded.

She pinned him with a look. "How serious are you about sticking this out?"

He didn't bat an eye. "I bought her a ring. I'm calling my mother tomorrow. I'm in this one hundred percent. As long as it takes."

Athena divided a look between them that

Pru couldn't interpret. "Fine. I'll back up the story."

"You will?"

"Do you really think I'm going to do anything to jeopardize Ari's placement here? She's ours. Mom wanted that. You got caught up in a shitty situation and made a choice. I can't say as it's the one I'd have made, and it's sure as shit not the one I'd expect from you. But you made it, you're in it, so I'll back you up."

Pru let out a long breath and, with it, some of the tension she'd been carrying around for the past couple of days. "Thank you. What about Kennedy and Maggie?"

"You leave Maggie to me."

"What will you tell her?"

"The trumped up, long-distance relationship version. She's going to lose her shit either way. She'll lose it less over that version. I'll talk her through it. Kennedy's on you. I'm guessing she's not gonna react particularly well to any of this."

"Probably not," Flynn agreed. "Xander may feel compelled to adjust my face with his fist."

Pru shook her head. "Don't be ridiculous."

"He warned me off you."

"He what? When?"

"That night at the bachelor party, after you went back inside."

"He *has* always had that brother vibe going toward you," Athena added.

"For God's sake, I'm a grown woman. Who I take to bed is none of his concern."

"I'm pretty sure none of us thought about you taking anybody to bed at all."

"Because good old, reliable Pru doesn't have a life." God that tasted bitter on her tongue.

"No. Because you're the most like Mom. Responsible and circumspect. You wouldn't take anyone who didn't matter, and we didn't know anyone did."

That mollified her—a little—even as it made her feel exposed. But Athena wasn't wrong. Flynn did matter. More than she wanted him to.

"Does that cover everything?" Athena asked.

"I suppose it does."

"Okay then. Ari, you can stop hovering outside the door. We know you're there."

Pru sighed. Of course, she was.

"Are y'all done, yet?"

"Yes, I think we are." One sister knew and the world hadn't ended. Maybe they'd get through this after all.

"Good, 'cause Athena promised me a game of *Redneck Life*."

"I want in on that," Flynn declared. "You owe me a rematch."

"Count me in, too. I've got just enough time for one round before my afternoon appointments." And there was nowhere she'd rather spend it than with her family.

"THERE'S my bouncing baby boy! It's been ages."

Flynn felt a trickle of guilt and was glad he hadn't engaged the video feed when he called his mother from the office computer. He usually made it a point to check in at least once a week, but he hadn't managed even once since he'd hit Eden's Ridge. "Sorry, Ma. How are things?"

"Oh, we're right as rain, we are. Your da and I are keeping Murphy and Tim, while Ciara and Mick are having a little holiday, just the two of them. Between you and me, I think they're trying for a girl to add to the mix this time."

Flynn had a moment to wish his engagement was real and that he'd be the one providing a granddaughter for his mother to spoil. She and Ari would be mad for one another. "And I'm sure you're entirely put out by the chance to be a doting gran all week."

His mother trilled with laughter. "Sure, and you know I'd tell them to stay a whole extra week for the chance. Your da's of a mind to teach the boys to fish, so they're off to the lake this afternoon. He'll be sorry he's missed you."

"I'm sorry to have missed him, too."

She continued to talk, filling him in on news about his assorted cousins, the neighbors, the staff, and more than half the village proper before she ran out of steam. "So, I want to hear all about you. Where are you calling from this time, my lad?" The faint clack of knitting needles punctuated the conversation. Flynn could imagine her in her sitting room, wool spilling over her lap as she settled in for a good chat.

"I'm still in Eden's Ridge."

"That's a long stay for you. Are you having a good visit with Kennedy, then?"

"Actually, she got married a couple of days after I got here."

"Married? Imagine that. I'm sure she made a lovely bride."

"She did. Her man suits her down to the ground. They're old sweethearts, as it turns out. Reconnected when she came home."

"Oh, and that's a lovely thing, to be sure. She always struck me as someone who needed some joy in her life."

"Well, she's found it. She's been beaming bright enough to beat the moon."

His mother gave a happy sigh. "I love a

happy ending. So, she's delaying her honey-moon or back already or—?"

"She and Xander are taking two weeks. They'll be back by the weekend."

"And you're still there?" There was no masking her curiosity.

"She and her sisters converted their family home into an inn. I'm sticking around to help out, while she's away."

"Sure, and that's a thoughtful wedding present. What's it like putting that hat back on?"

"A bit like riding a bike. But I'm not doing it for Kennedy."

"You're not?"

Flynn took a breath. "I met someone."

The clacking stopped. "Met someone? What? A woman?"

Her sincere shock wrangled a laugh. "Yes, a woman. Kennedy's sister, Pru."

She actually squealed with excitement. "Saints be praised! I have to tell your father."

"Hold on. Don't go get Da just yet."

"Is it not serious?"

Here was the decision he'd wrestled with all night and half the morning. Whether to tell her the lie or the truth. In the end, he couldn't give her anything less than honesty. "No, it's serious. It's just...it's complicated."

"Complicated how?" Her voice turned serious. "Flynn Michael Bohannon, is she married?"

"No. I have lines, Ma. That's not one I'd cross. No, she has a daughter. Well, foster daughter. She's in the process of adopting Ari." He briefly explained how Pru had gone from being sister to mother.

"The poor lamb. Both of them. Pru sounds a fine woman. Are you balking at being involved because of the child?"

"No. No, I adore Ari. It's just, we've found ourselves in something of a tight spot." He told the tale in as little detail as possible. He hadn't thought through the part about admitting to his mother he'd been sleeping with Pru. "So you'll be getting a call. And so will a lot of other people. References. Checking up on me. I need this to go well. I need to get through this background check so that things get back on track for Pru with the adoption."

His mother was silent for so long, he wondered if he'd lost the connection. "Ma?"

"You'd do all that for this woman?"

"It's my fault she's in this mess. She's had enough heartbreak losing her mother. I won't be responsible for her losing her child. So yes, I'll do whatever it takes."

He waited for her to throw his traveler lifestyle in his face, to remind him of all the reasons why this was insanity and wouldn't work.

"Well then, we'll do whatever we can to help. Tell me what you need."

Flynn loosed a breath, and with it a tension he hadn't been aware of holding. "Help thinking up six non-family references, to start. According to the paperwork, each of *them* will be asked to provide someone as a reference, as well."

They debated for near to an hour, but by the

end, he had his list of prospective references and their contact information.

"Thanks, Ma."

"You're a good boy, Flynn, with a good heart. I hope this Pru knows what she has in you."

"I do."

Flynn turned to see Pru in the doorway behind him. He waved her in.

"Is that her, then?"

"Yes, ma'am."

"Well and it's good to meet you, dear. I'm Moira Bohannon."

Pru slipped an arm around his shoulders. "And I'm very, very lucky you raised such a fine man."

"Son, I like this one. You should keep her."

Flynn chuckled. "I love you, Ma."

"I love you, too. And don't worry. Everyone in the village will hear the news by nightfall. I'll make your father take me down to the pub for supper."

"That'll do it for sure. Goodnight. And thanks."

"We'll talk again soon. Skype next time. I want to see your face."

Flynn ended the call and drew Pru close, enjoying the way she wrapped around him. "That's my side down. Now there's just Kennedy and Xander."

"And everyone else in town."

He tipped his head back to look at her. "You worried?"

"Less than I was. It's starting to feel like maybe we'll pull this off." She brushed her lips over his.

"Athena get off okay?"

"Yeah. She's going to call Maggie tonight, so I expect to be hearing from her later. I've got a full day of clients starting in an hour, and we've got three new check-ins coming this afternoon."

"I'll take care of them."

Pru smiled. "I know. Thanks."

Her easy acquiescence felt like a major victory.

"Why don't you pencil yourself in later tonight, after that phone call from your sister? I'll give *you* a massage."

"You really do have the best ideas."

"I've been known to have a few. Meanwhile, I'll be working on all of this." He gestured to the exception to policy packet.

"If you have any questions, you know where to find me." She pulled away and headed for the door. "And Flynn?"

"Yeah?"

She hesitated at the threshold, her expression turning serious. "Thank you. This means more to me than you can ever know."

As he watched her go, he realized he was starting to feel the same about her.

CHAPTER 9

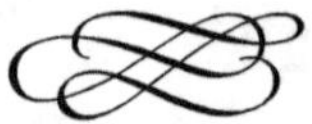

AT THE END OF a long day, Pru was dumping used linens from her massage practice into the washer, when Abbey pounced on her.

"Pru Reynolds, how dare you keep this a secret!"

Pru found herself pinned against the washing machine, her left hand held aloft, Abbey's own load of linens in a pile around their feet. "Jesus, girl, give me a heart attack, why don't you?"

"Heart attack my ass. Spill!" Abbey demanded.

This wasn't how she'd planned on the news getting out. But if she'd really wanted to keep it a secret, she wouldn't have put the ring back on when she was done with massages for the day. She just…liked it there. Tugging free of her friend's grip, Pru bent to gather up the mess in the floor and add it to the load. "So, I'm engaged."

"To *who?*"

"Flynn."

"I *knew* there was something going on between you two. But *engaged?* Isn't that kinda fast?"

She'd committed to the cover story now and found that it fell off her tongue with greater ease. "Two years isn't fast."

"Say what? But I thought—" Abbey waved a hand, dismissing whatever she was about to say. "Start at the beginning."

She did, giving Abbey the tale of how they'd supposedly met. The beauty of the scenario he'd concocted was that if they had met on that trip, she'd very likely have done exactly what he'd suggested. Because Flynn was…amazing. "Kennedy doesn't know anything about it, so we're trying to keep this quiet until we can tell her in person and explain."

"You can count on me. Man. *Engaged.*" Abbey pressed both fists to her mouth and danced in place. She was still dancing when Flynn stuck his head in the laundry room.

He went brows up. "Do I want to know?"

Pru just shook her head.

"Done for the day?" he asked.

"Only just."

"Good. Then you've got time for this."

"Time for what?"

Another head poked through the door. "Hey Pru."

"Porter. I wasn't expecting you." Even as she strode toward her foster brother, she stuck her left hand behind her back and began rotating the ring.

He caught her motion and grinned. "Don't

bother. Maggie told me."

Pru rolled her eyes. "Of course, she did. And are you here to give me the whole big brother routine in Xander's absence?"

"Nope. Not here about that at all." Wrapping his arms around her in a tight hug, he pressed a kiss to her brow. "Congratulations."

"That wasn't the word Maggie used."

"She'll calm down." Porter promised.

It was interesting that she'd called Porter to talk about it. "I didn't know you two were all talky talky these days."

"I wouldn't say we are. She just remembered why we used to be friends while she was here for the wedding. Speaking of, promise me you'll wait a bit to plan yours. I think another in a hurry wedding might send Maggie over the edge."

"I can promise I won't be planning a wedding any time soon." *There. A piece of truth.* "Now, why *are* you here?"

"Flynn called me."

"He did?" She glanced at the culprit for some kind of an explanation.

"I did. C'mon. You, too, Abbey. Your input would be useful for this." Flynn took Pru's hand and towed her toward the back door.

"Useful for what?" Pru asked.

"You'll see."

They all trooped out to the barn.

"What do you normally use this space for?" Flynn asked.

"It's been mostly storage for years. We cleaned out a lot, got rid of stuff to make room for the wedding."

"But there's not farm equipment that's coming back or anything?"

"No. This land hasn't been farmed in near to a century. Why?"

"Because I think that this could be your new day spa."

"A barn," Pru repeated.

"Bear with me. You've got mostly unused space out here. Now unless you plan on turning it into an event venue for more weddings like Kennedy's—"

"Please, God, no." Pru shuddered.

With a smile, Flynn squeezed her hand. "Then you have an opportunity here. You said you need space to set up for the kinds of services you and Abbey discussed. That means either adding onto the house or building something new elsewhere on the property, both of which would be of considerable expense. But if you were able to convert an existing space, then the idea comes back within reach. It's why I called Porter. To see what it would take to renovate the place."

Pru didn't even ask how Flynn knew Porter was a contractor. She could only suppose it came up at some point during the wedding. "You think we should turn the barn into a spa?"

"I think you want a spa, and it's a space you haven't considered."

Porter turned in a circle, his face assessing. "It's not a half bad idea. This thing was built back when things were built to last. Structure's solid, and I helped put on that tin roof myself about eight years back, so it's got decades more life in it." He began to pace. "The walls would need to be insulated and covered in drywall or maybe shiplap. You could either totally empty out the hay loft and make a second floor for treatment rooms or office space, or keep that for storage and just close it off. It *is* a barn, but you could absolutely play on that vibe. Sort of a rustic chic. Lots of reclaimed wood and stone accents."

As he talked, Pru began to see his vision, how it could be done. And she felt the first shoots of excitement begin to bloom.

"The beams could be left exactly as is—exposed. We'd add some better lighting for a sort of central atrium, with individual rooms off all sides. And I'm totally taking over your design without even asking what you'd want. What do you want, Pru?"

She took a few steps and looked at the space with fresh eyes. "I hardly know. This was mostly in pipe dream territory for way down the line. Everything you just said sounded awesome."

"What would you actually need for a day spa?" Porter asked.

"Abbey, this is more your territory than mine."

Face bright with interest, Abbey began to pace from one end to the other. "At least half a dozen treatment rooms. There's room for more on this first floor." She began to reel off prospective services, the necessary space and equipment requirements.

"How would we staff all of that?" Pru asked.

"You could do it one of two ways. Either hire people directly or set it up where the spa provides the facilities and equipment and charges basically a rental fee to practitioners, plus a percentage of their service costs."

"Like a booth rental in a beauty shop," Pru said.

"Exactly. That'd be the cheaper way to go. Let them be independent contractors, in charge of their own benefits and the like. The space rental would help cover renovation costs, and once that's paid for, you could always change the model as business grew. Most of the rooms could be customized as you were able to add more services."

"It could be done, *mo mhuirnín*," Flynn murmured.

Pru took a firm grip on her excitement before it could run wild. "Yeah, but for how much?"

Porter crossed his arms and gave the whole place a considering stare. "I'll have to work up an estimate. A lot of it could be done with re-claimed materials. Not a whole lot in that but sweat equity. The lion's share of cost will be la-bor, and you'll certainly get the family discount."

"Thanks for that."

"I'll put together some numbers, draw up some designs," he promised. "I know they have to pass Maggie, so I'll do two versions—a phased renovation that would allow you to start sooner and expand as business improved, and a whole shebang, all-at-once version. You pair that with a business plan, and I think you've got a good shot at making her agree to this. It'd be good for the town and good for the inn as a whole."

"Thank you, Porter."

"No problem." He looked to Flynn. "It's a good idea."

"The idea is all hers. I just saw a way to maybe make it happen sooner."

"Either way," Porter said. He stuck his hand out. "Welcome to the family, man."

Surprise flickered over Flynn's face before he shook. "Thank you."

"We should put our heads together about the business side of this," Pru said to Abbey. "Your extra treatments have been booking up. I think the interest is there."

"Definitely. I'll put my thinking cap on tonight. You wanna talk numbers tomorrow?"

"Yeah." Her mind already calculating outlay and service costs and prospective profit margins, Pru grinned. "Yeah, I do."

"You pull this off and I just might move home for good."

"Incentive!" Pru declared.

When they were alone, she turned and slipped her arms around Flynn. "Thank you."

"For what? All I did was point out a possibility."

"I would have put that off. I'd have told myself it was entirely out of reach and that it had to wait until a million other things were taken care of first, and I wouldn't have even asked."

"I know it's something that's important to you. It would make this family business more yours, I think, than what you have now. Certainly more to your interest. You deserve that."

"You've made me think a lot about the things I deserve, the things I want."

"Have I now?"

"I think maybe it's time you move into my room." Realizing he might like having his own space, she added, "If you want."

His eyes went hot and sharp. "Oh, I want.

But aren't you worried about the Coogan woman?"

With a wry smile Pru shrugged. "I'm pretty sure that ship has sailed and cannot get any worse. I don't know what's going to happen or how long we'll have. The fact is, I want you with me. I want to go to sleep with you and wake up next to you in the morning."

He skimmed a hand through her hair. "Your face would certainly be a fine thing to see of a morning on the pillow next to mine. Let's go get my stuff."

"Keep everything nice and loose. No, make sure your elbow is aimed directly at the floor." Flynn adjusted Ari's stance. "Better. Don't tuck your wrist in as you hold the fiddle. Straighten it out. There's a girl."

Ari reached for the bow.

"Not yet. You have to make sure you're holding things properly, while you get to know your strings. You're going to take your finger and pluck, like this." He demonstrated on his own fiddle, plucking the bottom string. "This is a G. Then D. Then A. Then E."

Ari followed suit.

"Good. Now each of these is tuned—"

"A fifth apart. I can hear that." The impatience simmering in her voice made him smile.

"That's right. Okay, pick up your bow."

She did, and he patiently corrected her hold.

"Good, now we're going to go with the G. You're going to place the bow on the string down by the frog."

"The what?"

"Down the bottom there, where the bowstrings are attached. That's it. Mind your elbow. Most of the action is in the wrist. You're going to play the G, drawing the bow down all the way to the tip." He demonstrated and she repeated. "Now the D going upbow. Then the A all the way down. Now the E all the way back up."

Ari mimicked his motions, drawing out a

shaky note from each string.

"Remember that the transition from one string to the next is a very small motion. You don't want to expend a lot of unnecessary energy. Try again. You're going for a clear, bright sound from each string."

She repeated the motions until she finally coaxed forth the tone he was looking for. "I did it!"

It was a small thing, but he felt an absurd amount of pride and pleasure at seeing her excitement. "You did indeed! Now—"

"Flynn!" Pru's shout echoed from the hallway.

He was half out of the family room, Ari on his heels, before he registered the tone as excitement rather than alarm. "What?"

She raced out of the office, eyes wide. "The whole house. They've booked the whole house."

"What?"

Pru took his hands and danced him in a circle. "I just got a booking for every remaining room in the house for *this weekend!*"

"You mean we're full up?" Ari asked.

"For the first time since we opened, other than the wedding. And none of these people are related to us or former fosters of Mom's!"

Ari whooped and did an impromptu dance of her own. Then she stopped. "Wait a minute. But we were airing everything out and in the middle of that deep clean. Almost none of the beds are made."

"And everybody will be showing up for the jam session at six," Flynn added. Perhaps today hadn't been the best time to try making that a more regular thing.

"I know," Pru said. "We've got a thousand things to do. It's a group of women from Nashville coming for a girls' weekend. They were already packed when they called, so they'll be here in four hours."

"How will we get everything done?" Ari asked.

"Divide and conquer," Flynn told her.

They made a list, prioritizing tasks and assigning them via time-honored tradition: Rock.

Paper. Scissors. When Ari's rock crushed Flynn's scissors and he got stuck scrubbing toilets and cleaning showers, he accepted it with considerably more good humor than he ever had when he lost to his sister. He'd hated this duty more than anything growing up and had often spent the time honing his cursing skills. By the time he'd turned eighteen, he'd developed astounding proficiency and creativity in that arena.

He hauled the caddy of cleaning supplies up to the third floor and waited for the resentment and irritation to kick in. It didn't. Instead, as he moved from room to room, he found himself lifting his voice in song, testing the acoustics of each bathroom. He was cleaning bathrooms and singing. His mother would be immediately checking him for a fever, maybe calling up Dr. O'Dwyer. But it just didn't feel the same. Instead of that envy of the very guests he prepared for, he felt an odd satisfaction. It was different with Pru. Everything was different with Pru. He was contented here in a way he'd never imagined he could be.

Hearing her laughter, Flynn went to the window and looked out. She and Ari were gathering sheets from the line. It was a thing he'd seen his own mother do a thousand times and never thought a thing about, but he found himself staring as they worked to neatly fold the sheet. Pru added the square to the basket, then stroked a hand down Ari's hair. The girl tipped her head to Pru's shoulder, one arm around her waist, as the two of them looked off toward the mountains. The quiet moment hit him right in the gut.

He wanted this. With Pru. All of it. Ari, the inn, the life he'd fallen into. Not for the next few weeks or months, until the threat of Ari being taken was over. He wanted them for real. He wanted to make this home. Because he was in love with them both.

He was down the stairs and striding off the back porch before he could think better of it. They were back to the sheets.

"Ari, you may want to cover your eyes," Flynn told her.

"Why?"

"Because I need to kiss your mother."

He didn't wait to see if she did, instead diving his hands into Pru's hair and laying his mouth over hers. Over the past weeks, he'd felt so many things for this woman. A driving need to possess. A devastating gentleness. An unwavering fascination. Here was something else altogether—a quiet homecoming that vibrated down to his very marrow. Perfect harmony. Flynn reveled in it, in her, as he sank into the kiss and gathered her close. Her hands fisted in his shirt, sheet and all, as her mouth opened under his on a quiet sigh.

He wanted the moment to go on forever. But he remembered they had things to do and an avid audience of one, so he eased back, pressing his brow to hers.

Pru trembled a little in his arms. "Wha... what was that for?"

Because I love you. The words were right

there, waiting to spill out. But making that announcement while laundry billowed around them was hardly his style. Such a declaration merited more forethought on the method of delivery. That should matter nearly as much as the words themselves the first time they were spoken.

"I saw you from the window. You made such a pretty picture, I had to come down."

Pru tipped her face back, one dark brow raised. "The sight of clean laundry had you overcome with amorous intent?"

Flynn raised her hands to his lips and smiled. "Just you."

"Smitten," Ari declared. "The word you're looking for is smitten."

"Quite." With reluctance, he let her go and stepped back. "I'll get back to my cleaning. I just needed that to tide me over."

Whistling, he turned his back on them both—Pru staring and Ari grinning from ear to ear—and headed back inside to plan.

CHAPTER 10

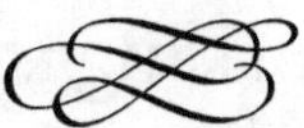

"SO I SAID, DEANNA, we had a party when you married the bastard. We should have a party for cutting him loose," Wendy declared. Or was it Jasmine? Pru had lost track.

"The divorce was officially filed this morning, so here we are," the newly single Deanna announced.

Pru topped off the woman's wine. "Congratulations on your new freedom."

The group of ten women from Nashville had arrived mere minutes after they'd finished prepping the rooms. Flynn had appointed himself bag boy and cheerfully hauled luggage up to the assigned rooms, chatting and flirting the whole way, while Pru and Ari were plating hors d'oeuvres and uncorking some wine. At least three of the women practically swooned on the spot. Not that Pru could blame them. Flynn was sexy as hell on an average day, and when he laid on that Irish charm, no woman could resist him, as evidenced by the fact that Deanna had tried to invite him to drop by her room later.

"Sorry about propositioning your man," she said. "If my ex had been anything like him, we wouldn't be having a divorce party this weekend. Came right out and said he was engaged and started singing your praises. You are one lucky woman."

Pru couldn't stop the smug smile that curved her lips. "I certainly am."

"I hope you won't be offended if we look," one of the others added.

"He's so very pretty," another sighed.

Pru laughed. "Yes, he is. And look all you

like. There will be a few other handsome faces available for your ogling pleasure in the next little bit. Flynn and a bunch of other local musicians will be having a jam session out back this evening."

"Yeah? What sort of music?" Deanna asked.

"A little of this, a little of that. Bluegrass, country, Irish…a lot will depend on who happens to show up this week."

"Oh, is it a regular thing?" Wendy asked.

"We're trying it out this summer. Feel free to take your wine and canapés outside to enjoy."

Ari stuck her head in the room. "Hey Mom, we have incoming."

Pru froze in the process of uncorking another bottle of wine. Mom. Ari had just called her Mom. Emotion swelled in her throat 'til she thought she might just dissolve into a puddle of goo.

Ari frowned. "You okay?"

Pru swallowed. "Fine. I'm fine. Incoming what, baby?"

"Locals. Looks like word got out about our

jam session. People are parking along the drive and hauling in coolers and lawn chairs."

As the Nashville girls began to make their way outside, Pru headed to the front of the house and peered out.

"Good Lord. They're all the way to the street."

Ari peeked out the sidelight on the other side of the door. "Well, at least they're bringing their own snacks. I don't think we have anywhere near enough to feed that many people."

"Indeed, we do not." If they continued to make this a regular event, she really needed to find out if there were any kind of special permits they needed. "But people are good."

"People are good," Ari agreed.

By the time the musicians began the opening set, the entire backyard looked like a giant picnic. People sat in chairs or sprawled on quilts around the makeshift stage. Flynn had finally taken down the lights from the wedding and strung them across the yard, lending a festive feel to the gathering. Pru circulated, greeting locals, chatting with guests. The whole thing felt more like a party than work.

"We're about to take a little break shortly, but I wanted to end this first set with a song for our lovely hostess. Can we get a round of applause for Pru Reynolds?"

The ripple of applause was punctuated by a few whistles and whoops. Pru felt her cheeks heat and was grateful the sun was fading.

Flynn swapped his fiddle for a guitar and looked right at her. "I've been working on turning what I feel for you into a melody. I don't know as this quite does it justice, but it's the best I've got." He began to strum.

Pru curled a hand around the porch rail as she felt her knees go weak. His voice wrapped around her like velvet, and everyone else melted away as he crooned the sweetest words she'd ever heard—words of love and home and forever. Words that embodied everything she wanted, everything she needed. He kept his eyes fixed on hers. She couldn't read them from this distance, but her heart stumbled nonetheless.

Was he saying he really loved her? God, it felt like it. It felt like this performance was for her and her alone. With a pang of grief, Pru dismissed that as wishful thinking. He was a performer. An exceptionally gifted one, who was only playing the part they'd agreed on. He wanted these people to believe that he loved her and wanted to marry her. That's all it was.

But she wanted. As the last notes died way, as his eyes lingered on hers, she felt the pull between them. She felt the undeniable connection she'd forged with this man. On some level, despite the extraordinary circumstances, it was real. Wasn't it?

"Well that's it. I have to hate you." Deanna's voice broke into Pru's reverie.

"I'm sorry, what?"

"There's just no justice in the world. There is a man like *that* out there and you're the one who's going to marry him."

"You're going to *what?*"

Pru whirled to find her sister and Xander standing half a dozen feet away, mouths agape. *Oh shit.* "Kennedy! You're back! We weren't expecting you until tomorrow." She knew her voice was way too bright, but she couldn't think, couldn't do anything but stare. This was not how she'd wanted to present the news.

Kennedy zeroed in on her left hand, lifting it to study the ring. "Lucy, you got some 'splainin' to do." The joking words did nothing to lighten the serious expression.

"I—" Jesus, what could she say?

Flynn had worked his way through the crowd. "Welcome back."

The hand he slid around her waist settled the explosion of nerves in her belly. They were in this together. They'd get through it together. Even if Xander was looking at Flynn's hand like he was considering taking it off at the wrist.

"Why don't we take this inside?" Flynn suggested.

Ari came flying across the porch. "Kennedy!"

Kennedy absorbed the enthusiastic hug. "Hey baby girl. Missed you."

"Missed you, too." Ari stepped back to slip an arm around Pru, beaming up at Flynn. "Isn't this awesome?"

"It's something," Xander said.

"Love is in the air," she sang. "Flynn's teaching me to play the fiddle. And check it, everybody loves the new Friday night jam session. Isn't it great? You should sit down and listen." Her words came in a torrent of enthusiasm that could only be managed by a teenager.

Pru laid a hand on Ari's shoulder. "I'm sure they will after the break. We need to step inside for a bit to give them the update. Could you keep an eye on things out here, sweetheart?"

"'Kay!"

None of them spoke as they wove their way through the crowd and into the house.

As soon as Pru shut the door to the family study, Kennedy rounded on them. "What the *hell*, y'all? *Engaged?* We've been gone for *two weeks.* Two weeks. Half a month. Fourteen days. A fortnight, even. Are you insane?"

Hearing the timeline hammered on like that was epic splash of reality. They'd been living in this fantasy world, where everything felt like it had taken much longer than it really had. Put like that, in a tone just shades away from outrage, Pru remembered anew why this scheme was nuts.

"It's not what you think," she began.

"Then please, tell me how you haven't both lost your freaking minds."

"Watch it, *deifiúr beag.*" A faint edge rode beneath Flynn's easy tone.

Pru took a breath and decided to say it fast, like ripping off a Band-Aid. "It all started when I decided to seduce Flynn."

Kennedy stared. "When you did what now?"

"You heard me."

"I heard you, but I'm having trouble believing it."

Pru bristled. "Is it so hard to believe I have

interest enough in an attractive man and the confidence to do something about it?"

"Well, I just…I never thought—"

"Right. You never thought. No one ever thinks about me because I'm the responsible, dependable one, who can always be counted on to do anything anybody needs because I have no life."

Kennedy paused in her pacing, distress interrupting her disbelief. "We don't think that, Pru."

"You do. All of you do. And why shouldn't you? That's been me most of my life. That will be me for most of the rest of it, probably, because Ari will come first. She does come first, and I don't regret that choice for a second. But I just wanted one thing for myself. I wanted Flynn." Seeing Xander's ears turning red, she rolled her eyes. "I'll spare you the gory details, Xander. Suffice it to say we have an adult relationship."

He held up a hand. "None of my business.

But how the hell did you get from an affair to *marriage* in two weeks?"

"There were…extenuating circumstances."

Xander narrowed his eyes in the cop stare meant to intimidate. "Tell me what kind of extenuating circumstances lead to a proposal."

"It wasn't a proposal," Pru said. "Not exactly. It was very bad timing with the arrival of Ari's new social worker." As Flynn slipped his hand into hers, she filled them in as succinctly as possible.

"Why didn't you just say you wouldn't be getting married until after the adoption was finalized, and he'd be living elsewhere in the meantime?" Kennedy asked.

Pru opened her mouth to speak, then closed it again. That possibility had never even crossed her mind.

"We panicked," Flynn said. "And either way, we're much too far down this road to back out now."

"Who else knows the truth?" Xander asked.

"Athena," Pru said.

"And Maggie?" Kennedy asked.

"Athena thought she'd handle the long-distance relationship version better."

Kennedy pinched the bridge of her nose. "I am way too jet lagged for this conversation."

Pru just wanted a chance to regroup. How could she have gone from that glorious, heady feeling of being swept away...to this? "I'm sure you'll want to discuss it more later, but we have guests we need to see to."

"I need to be getting back out there for the second set."

"Go ahead. I'll be along in a minute."

Flynn's eyes lingered on hers, a silent question of whether she'd be all right alone with them. That was very much debatable, but she needed to face this, and someone had to deal with their guests. She squeezed his hand. With a faint nod, he slipped out the door.

Across the room, Kennedy dropped into a chair. "Pru, I don't even know what to say about all this."

"Look, I know it's a shock, and it's not ideal, but—"

"Ideal? No. It's a clusterfuck. We're going to have to lie to the social worker. If she finds out…"

Xander laid a hand on her shoulder. "Hey."

"I am aware of the stakes, Kennedy," Pru snapped. "If you think I haven't worried myself sick over the whole thing, you'd be wrong."

"It's not just that she could take Ari away. It's the situation. Honey, I'm worried about you. Flynn is the kind of guy you've spent your whole life avoiding for very good reasons. What's this going to do to you when it's over? You've been down this road before, and it damn near killed you."

Pru opened her mouth to say it wasn't the same, but the door swung open and Ari barged in. "Flynn's going to stick."

She was too speechless at the utter conviction in Ari's voice to chastise her for eavesdropping…again. Fresh worry bloomed. They hadn't talked about this, not since the beginning.

Maybe that was a mistake on her part. Maybe she should have kept reiterating the transient nature of their circumstances instead of letting herself get carried away by the fantasy.

"Honey, you understand that this is temporary, right?" That felt more real now that Kennedy and Xander had burst their happy little bubble. "As soon as things are finalized, Flynn's going to leave." Because that's what men like him did. Like her father. That's what Kennedy was implying. The idea of it had a pit yawning in her stomach.

Ari shrugged, apparently unimpressed with the argument. "Maybe. But his first reaction to this whole thing was to marry you. Think about that." And on that note, she walked back out.

FLYNN HAD NEVER WANTED a performance to be over with more than the jam session that night. So, of course, it ran long, with guests and townsfolk lingering and socializing.

Kennedy and Xander stuck around for a bit, listening, visiting with locals, and Pru had been a little bit dimmer for their presence. Now that he'd had the chance to see her without it, he recognized the shell she'd worn when he first met her—or maybe it was really armor. She'd pulled into herself in the face of Kennedy and Xander's disapproval, and Flynn hated it. He hated seeing the worry back in her eyes.

At the end of the night, after Ari had crashed and the Nashville girls had been poured into bed—literally in the case of a few of them—Pru still moved around the kitchen, putting together a massive casserole for the next morning's breakfast. "Deanna's booked a massage tomorrow, and I need to get up with Abbey to see if she's willing and able to come in for a group facial for the Nashville girls. We'll need to clean up from tonight's shindig, of course." She continued to ramble on about anything and everything except how things went with Kennedy and Xander.

At last, Flynn simply stepped into her path and wrapped his arms around her. "Breathe."

On a shuddering breath, Pru burrowed in, leaning against him. "God, Flynn. This is not how I wanted this to come out. I wanted to explain it to them in a controlled fashion, make them see the logic of it. And instead…"

"It will be all right." If it was within his power to grant, he'd make sure of it.

She tipped her head up to look at him, those dark eyes brimming with anxiety. "How will it? For our plan to work, they have to agree to it. They have to be willing to lie for us. You saw them."

"They're worried about the situation—rightly so. And Kennedy is legitimately worried about you." Flynn hesitated. "What did she mean you've been down this road before?" Pru stiffened, and he rushed to explain. "I saw Ari hiding and started to come back to talk to her about it. I heard the last bit of your conversation when she went into the room."

Her expression shuttered and she stepped

away from him. It was such a contrast to the warmth he'd grown used to with her, he almost rubbed his arms as if against a chill. A new knot of anxiety curled in his gut. "What aren't you telling me?"

"It was forever ago. It doesn't matter now."

"Obviously Kennedy thinks it does. What's she talking about, *agra?*"

"My father."

Whatever he'd expected her to say, it wasn't that. "Your father? I don't understand. What does that have to do with me?"

Pru sucked in a breath and let it out in a gush. "Because you're exactly his type. The type I have spent my entire life avoiding getting involved with."

"What type is that?"

"A born gypsy. He was an actor with an on-the-road theater troupe. Handsome, a brilliant performer, with the itchiest feet you've ever seen. And I worshiped the ground he walked on. So did my mother—until she got pregnant. I don't remember her. She'd been an actress with the troupe, or so I was told. My coming along ruined an up and coming career. As soon as she was able, she disappeared and left me with my father. I was barely more than an infant."

Jesus Christ. He'd heard the sad story of Kennedy's birth parents and how her own mother had abandoned her when she was little. There were, she'd told him, a lot of similar stories among her sisters and foster siblings. No one ended up in the system without a sad story. But a baby. How could a woman be so cold?

"Daddy loved me, in his way, but being a parent was never his first priority. It often wasn't even his last. The only reason he managed to keep me as long as he did was because the entire troupe sort of shared care-taking duty of me. But people rotated in and out of it, depending on the show. Some were more kid-friendly than others. Most agreed the road was not the best place for a child. Eventually, there was no one willing to look after me but Daddy."

She paused, knitting her hands together in a restless gesture that betrayed far more upset about this than her matter-of-fact tone conveyed. "I was left behind twice before social services got involved and took me away."

"Left behind?" Flynn demanded.

"He forgot me. The first time was only a couple of hours. I'd been playing in the theater dressing room, and he thought I was already on the bus when they rolled out. The second time, I fell asleep during the after party. It was late, after midnight, and I'd found a quiet spot to curl up and sleep. I didn't wake up until morning, and the theater was dark and empty."

"How old were you?"

"Seven."

Appalled, Flynn wanted to gather her up, but he sensed she needed the distance, just now. "You must've been terrified."

"Beyond. I made it up to the front lobby and beat on the front doors until my hands were bruised." She looked at them now, as if she could still see the bruises. "Eventually, a woman walking her dog saw me and called the police. The bus rolled up about the time they got the door open. My father was beside himself. They wouldn't turn me over to him. Social services was called. They set up a court date to establish his fitness as a parent, and I was put into my first foster home."

As she spoke, her voice went flatter and flatter. He'd only thought she'd been shut down before. "It was just supposed to be temporary, until the hearing. The troupe had to move on. They had a show scheduled and couldn't afford to miss it. He went with them because his understudy was ill, and no one else could play the part. Everybody's paycheck depended on it. He promised me he'd come back as soon as it was done. But as it happens, at that show, he finally got the big break he'd been waiting for all those years. So, he didn't show for the court hearing, and I came to Joan."

"And that's it? He didn't fight for you?"

"Oh, he made a few grand gestures over the years. Promises he usually broke. But he always left in the end. His dreams were more important than me."

"He sounds a right bastard. What kind of a man walks away from his child? What kind of man *forgets* his child?" Ari had only been in his life for a matter of weeks, and he couldn't fathom not thinking of her every day for the rest of his life.

"A selfish one." The matter-of-fact tone held no judgment. This was her truth. She was simply stating it. Flynn could see her struggling to pull herself back from whatever dark place the recitation had dragged her to. "You're not selfish. My father would never have done what you're doing. He'd have found some excuse, some way of slipping out of it. You may have a gypsy's soul, Flynn, but you're *not* like my father. You're a far better man."

"I'm not sure the bar's too high for being a better man than he was. I'm sorry for how he hurt you." The words felt wholly inadequate in the face of what she'd endured. He could see now why she was so fiercely determined to put Ari first, to maintain the home that had been given to her by Joan, and he felt himself slide a little deeper in love with her.

Pru shrugged. "It doesn't matter now. I'm a grown woman, and I made my own choice to be with you. I don't regret it."

"Kennedy seems to think you will." That stung. They'd been friends for years, and he'd thought she knew him better than that.

"She's not factoring the most salient point."

"What's that?"

"I don't expect you to stay."

The words, her obvious belief in them, were a slap in the face. Flynn wanted to argue, to make the declaration he'd been trying to make with the song he'd sung before the entire night had gone off the rails. But in her current frame of mind, would she believe him? She had reasons, good ones, not to trust people to stick around. Both her parents had left her. Kennedy had left for years, and though the reasons hadn't been what Pru and her sisters had thought, the emotional toll was bound to be the same. Even Athena and Maggie had gone off to their own lives across the country, trusting that she'd be what she'd always been. The one who stayed.

She needed someone to stay for her. Flynn wanted to be that man. Above and beyond the untenable position they were in with the phony engagement, he wanted a life with her. This life. But he understood that Pru was a woman who'd put little stock in words and promises. Too many people had broken them. He needed to prove himself through actions, and that would simply take time.

So instead of making professions, Flynn stepped into her, cupping her face in his hands. "I'm here. Whatever may come, I'm here. I won't leave you to face any of this alone." *I won't leave you.*

When she sighed, some of the tension seemed to leech out of her. "Take me to bed, Flynn."

If this was all she'd take from him for now, he'd give her everything he had. He led her back to the bedroom, where they quietly undressed.

Here was tenderness and a bottomless well of patience as he took her up and over the first peak. And if, as they slid over the edge together with sighs and moans, he gave her the words in Irish, she was too lost in sensation to ask. But he held the words, and her, close to his heart, as they both drifted off to sleep.

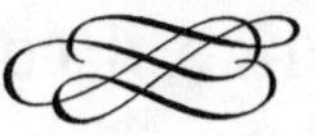

THEY GOT THROUGH THE weekend, giving the Nashville girls a true pampering experience. When she'd mentioned the possibility of expanding to a full day spa, they'd been all over the idea, insisting on getting on the mailing list for when it happened. When Porter brought by the initial concept drawings Sunday night, it seemed like a sign. Or maybe Pru just wanted to cling to the idea that she could do something to distract Kennedy from the situation with Flynn.

In the past few days, Kennedy had kept her

distance. It had been under the guise of getting over jet lag and unpacking from their honeymoon, but the fact that Kennedy had been a world traveler for a decade made it feel like evasion and avoidance. Pru had felt her disapproval radiating from the house she shared with Xander three miles away. Standing on their front porch, she hesitated over the knocker. The police cruiser was gone, so Xander was on duty. Pru was grateful. One set of disapproving eyes was enough. Still, maybe it was a mistake to do this now.

Before she could make up her mind, the door swung open.

"Hey." Kennedy sounded surprised to see her.

"Hi." Pru dropped the hand she'd lifted to knock. "Were you on your way out?"

"I was thinking about a walk."

"It's a bad time. I can come back later." She took a step back, already regretting coming over.

"Pru. Please don't." Kennedy stepped forward and wrapped her in a hug. "I don't want to fight."

"Neither do I." Much as she wanted to, Pru couldn't quite let herself tuck her head and return the embrace. She was still feeling tender after Kennedy's accusations.

"Please come inside." To settle the matter, Kennedy took Pru's hand and dragged her through the door. "You want a glass of tea? Some coffee?"

"I'm fine." Pru laid the envelope with Porter's drawings on the counter. Impatience simmered, but she knew she couldn't just jump right into business. Other things had to be said first. "Look, Kennedy, I'm sorry. I know you don't approve of my being involved with Flynn—"

"It's not that. Who you take to your bed is none of my business. I'll admit to being shocked as hell because of your history. I never would have put you with Flynn. But he's a good man or I wouldn't be friends with him. I'm just upset at the potential ramifications for Ari."

"So am I. So is he. She's our first priority."

"I get that. And that's why Xander and I will support you however we need to."

Pru released a breath and felt her knees go rubbery with relief. After their reaction on Friday, she hadn't been sure what they'd do. "Thank you."

"But—"

Of course, there was a but.

"Where does that leave you?"

"What do you mean?"

"I'm still worried about what this relationship is going to do to you in the end. I love Flynn like a brother. But he's got a way bigger case of wanderlust than I ever had. At least in my travels, I stayed for a few weeks or months at a time in one place. He stays days."

And yet even before Lydia Coogan, he'd wanted to stay for longer than those few days.

"You know one side of him. You know the gypsy. But that's not all he is." Pru thought of the man she'd come to depend on over the past few weeks. The one who was an unfailingly generous lover. The one who noticed the little things and made thoughtful gestures that continually surprised her. The one who'd upended his entire life to right an inadvertent wrong.

Kennedy's smile was pained around the edges. "Not all, no. But at the core, he's different than I was. I came back because I had roots. He's always felt strangled by them. Nothing's going to change that."

Pru bit back a bitter retort. Nothing was going to change that. Meaning no one. Meaning her. Because she wasn't good enough. She wasn't worth staying for. And wasn't that just par for the course? Everyone left her.

But in her heart of hearts, she couldn't believe that about Flynn. She couldn't reconcile Kennedy's view of him with her own experiences. She'd continually reminded herself he would leave, that he'd resent the position he'd been forced into by circumstance. And at every turn, he'd proven faithful and true. The steady partner she so desperately wanted rather than the gypsy everyone believed him to be. She'd seen him settle in, settle down, seen him change since he arrived. He felt more than simple lust and responsibility. She knew he did. In many ways, she'd given him the home he'd clearly been looking for, whether he realized it or not.

And even as she knew Kennedy would call her a fool, a part of her believed that maybe they could make this work for real. The certainty of it blew through Pru, smoothing the edges roughened by her sister's return. She had faith in Flynn. Faith in what they brought to each other, in what they made together. So, in the end, they'd see. But for right now, she wanted to change the subject.

"I didn't come here to discuss Flynn. I came to talk about the inn."

"Is there a problem? Did something go wrong, while we were away?"

"The inn's fine. You know I talked to Abbey about offering some freelance services, while she was in town."

"Sure. How's that going?"

"Like gangbusters. More business than she

can reasonably handle. My massage schedule has stayed booked almost solid. If Flynn hadn't pitched in and taken over some of the inn keeping duties, I don't know how I would have managed while you were gone."

"Wait, Flynn's been *working* at the inn?"

"Seamlessly. He's great at it."

Shock rippled over Kennedy's features before she waved it away. "I'm sorry for not being here, for not realizing I was leaving you in the lurch with having to manage my brainchild on top of your own established business, by yourself.

Pru just shook her head. "That's not my point. The point is, there have been dozens of queries through the website about more. I think we have a reasonable market for a day spa."

"A day spa." Kennedy kicked back against the counter, a considering look on her face. "I admit I gave it a little thought when we moved your massage studio into the house, but we were so busy getting everything renovated and up and running, I hadn't gone any further than that."

"Abbey and I have been working on a plan." Pru pulled out the sheaf of papers she'd brought, showing the list of prospective services and price lists and estimated business, based on the interest from the past couple of weeks. "Like the original business plan you wrote up for the inn, this could be ramped up as income allowed."

"But what about space? Other than your studio and the family spaces, the rest of the house is entirely devoted to the inn."

"That's the other thing I came to talk to you about." She pulled out the first of the drawings. "I had Porter put these together based on the ideas Abbey and I had. This is how we could renovate the barn. He's already sent over initial estimates on cost, and I'm working on crunching the numbers to show how fast we could pay for it through a couple of different business models."

Kennedy slowly scanned the drawings.

"This is amazing. He could really do this with our *barn?*" She gave a little laugh. "What am I saying? It's Porter. Of course, he can do this with our barn."

"It was Flynn's idea to use the space. I was thinking some kind of addition way on down the line. But using the barn would put this much closer to achievable. And the income from the spa would help offset those times when the inn itself isn't full."

"It's a good idea, Pru."

"I know." She had faith in it because Flynn had faith in her. "I want to propose it to Maggie and Athena as the next phase. I need your help solidifying the business plan before I present it."

"You're the one who supported me in the idea of an inn to begin with. Of course, I'll support you in this. But do you really want to do this now? While everything hangs in the balance with Ari?"

"The situation with Ari is going to be a lot of hurry up and wait. I'm worried enough about the whole thing—I need something to distract me. This will do it, and it's something that will ultimately benefit the entire family."

Kennedy gave her a long study before finally nodding. "Okay. I'm starting back to work at the tavern tonight, but if you can hook me up with the numbers you and Abbey have run, and the rest of it, I can get started converting all of that to a business plan that will justify how we'd pay for the renovation, based on Porter's calculations."

"Thank you. I'll start putting out feelers for other prospective service providers. Having a list of potential staff should also weigh in our favor."

"Maggie does love having all the details worked out," Kennedy agreed.

They lapsed into silence. That was her cue to go. "I need to be getting back. We're still turning rooms from this weekend, and I've got clients booked all afternoon." She headed for the door.

"Pru?"

She turned back to see Kennedy watching her with concern.

"Are we okay?"

Were they? Probably not. No matter what she said, Kennedy was going to believe that her relationship with Flynn was a bad idea. Nothing but time and having things settled with Ari was going to change her mind. But this was a step in the right direction.

"I think we will be. I love you, sis. Welcome home."

You are going to the special hell, Flynn thought. Surely that was the penalty for lying to a man of the cloth. Yet here he was, sitting across from Reverend Hodgson, with a pot of fresh coffee and a plate of cookies between them, as he accepted congratulations on his engagement.

"I was just so surprised when Crystal mentioned it," the reverend said.

"Crystal?" Flynn asked.

"Crystal Blue, the owner of the diner," he explained. "She was out here Friday night for the music."

"Oh right." By now, everyone in town knew. Even the checker at the grocery store had offered her felicitations. Flynn was just having a little trouble keeping up with all the connections.

"Anyway, Pru's been part of the congregation for such a long time now, and she never breathed a word."

"We kept the whole thing quiet. A lot of people wouldn't have understood the long-distance thing."

"I'm sure it was extremely difficult."

"It was," Flynn agreed. Was hell a finite level of suck and torture or was he adding to his punishment with every additional lie?

"Well," Reverend Hodgson lifted his coffee in a toast, "love will find a way."

"To be sure," Flynn agreed.

"I'm so pleased for you both. Pru's a good

woman, and it's a wonderful thing to see her happy."

"She's the best woman I know. These past weeks with her have been the best of my life. I wouldn't trade them for anything." At least he could be honest about that.

"Many more good years to come. When is the wedding?"

"Oh, well, we haven't discussed it yet. Our focus at the moment is on Ari and getting through all the necessary formalities for me to be approved as a foster parent. We don't want to delay that process any further than necessary. Besides, Kennedy's is only just past, and I think we could all use a little breathing room before we go down that path again."

"My what is just past?" The woman herself strode into the kitchen. "Hey, Reverend."

"Kennedy, my dear, welcome home. Flynn and I were just discussing his engagement to your sister. It's so wonderful that two of you found happiness so close together. Joan would be so pleased."

Kennedy's smile looked a little forced. "I wish she could have been there for my wedding."

"I know she was there in spirit." He squeezed her hand.

Flynn sipped some of his own coffee and cleared his throat. "I was just telling the good Reverend here that Pru and I aren't setting a date until after things are sorted with Ari."

"That is the plan," Kennedy agreed.

"Perfectly sensible. It's so wonderful what y'all are doing for that child."

"It's what Mom would have wanted."

"What about you, Flynn? Are you ready to be a father?"

Was he ready? Flynn weighed his words carefully. "I don't know that any man is ever truly ready for that responsibility. But Ari is a bright, talented girl and an easy child to love. I'll certainly make every effort to do right by her."

Reverend Hodgson beamed. "That's a good attitude to have."

"Where is she, anyway?" Kennedy asked.

"I dropped her at the farm this morning. Logan's teaching her to ride. I'm pretty sure she's completely besotted with his chestnut mare. When I left, she was working on negotiating a trade of lessons for mucking stalls."

Kennedy made a face. "She *must* be besotted then. What about Pru?"

"She went in for a ninety-minute massage with a client a bit ago. I'm sorry she's not available to see you, Reverend."

"Quite all right. I'm sure I'll see y'all again Sunday."

"Yes, sir. Were you okay with the piece I emailed you about for the next offertory?" Flynn figured he might as well do whatever he could to rack up some points with the Almighty.

"Oh absolutely. Everybody so loved what you played last week. We're all looking forward to it." The minister drained the last of his coffee and pushed back from the kitchen table. "I won't keep y'all. I know you've got a business to run, and I've got other congregants to see. I just wanted to stop by and offer my congratulations."

Flynn rose. "We appreciate it."

"Kennedy, it's good to have you home. Will we be seeing you and Xander on Sunday?"

"Now that we're past the jet lag, absolutely."

Flynn saw the reverend out. When he got back to the kitchen, Kennedy had poured her own cup of coffee and was nibbling on a cookie.

"I'm glad I caught you while Pru was tied up. I wanted to talk to you."

Flynn tensed. "Is this the part where you reef me for getting involved with your sister?"

"No. You're both single, consenting adults. Given her history, you aren't the kind of guy I'd have put her with. But it's not my choice. Concerns about Pru's emotional wellbeing aside, I wouldn't have a problem with this at all, if not for how it could impact Ari."

"We're doing everything we can to rectify that situation."

"I know. I know you are. And I appreciate that more than I can say. But you've stuck this out for weeks now. You've endured the background checks and other invasions of your privacy. It wouldn't be a shock at all if you realized that this was all more than you were prepared to deal with."

Flynn narrowed his eyes. "What are you saying?"

"I'm saying you can break off this farce of an engagement no harm, no foul. The social worker isn't going to hold that against Pru. Maybe the woman will think poorly of you, but you won't be around for that to matter. Then things go back to exactly what they were meant to be, with Pru finishing the home study and adoption, and you can get back to your life."

He stared at her. "That simple?"

Kennedy spread her hands. "That simple. You both panicked and overcomplicated the situation. But there's no need for the charade."

Because, of course, she couldn't see it as anything more than that. She couldn't imagine a circumstance where this was what he truly wanted. "So I'm just to walk away like everyone else in her life? I'm supposed to be the man who can do that, after promising I'd stand by her through all of this?"

"It was a promise made under extreme circumstances. She'll understand."

The genuine kindness and empathy in Kennedy's expression had temper flaring. She honestly thought she was saving him here. "Fuck that. I'm not walking out on her. I'm not going to walk away from responsibility like her father did."

Kennedy blinked. "She told you about him?"

"She did. And about your less than flattering comparison between us."

Kennedy shook her head. "I didn't mean it like that. I'm just worried about the situation. I know you went into this with the best of intentions, but you're not really prepared to stay here for real, and I have to think about what that's going to do to her, and to Ari when you're gone."

He didn't know which part pissed him off more. That she didn't seem to think he could find Pru important enough to stick for or that she legitimately thought he could take this escape clause she was offering with any kind of a clear conscience. "What if I am prepared to stay?"

"You're not serious. You've never wanted to stay anywhere, ever."

That had been true for more years than Flynn cared to admit. But didn't a man have the right to change? Didn't he deserve an opportunity to be more than what he'd been? To be different? "Maybe I want this. Did you ever think of that? Maybe it suits me. *She* suits me. I've slipped back into this life, and in some ways, it's like I never left it. The good parts, the parts I'm good at, like seein' to guests' comfort and makin' them feel at home. And not the bad parts, like feelin' like I never had a choice about my own future."

"Flynn, you left this life because you didn't

want it. You told me that yourself, time and time again."

Was this what Pru felt, fighting to be something other than what her sisters had always believed her to be? This chafing of everyone's expectations against her own desires? "Did you ever stop to think that maybe it's different for me now, as a grown ass man, to make the choice?" That was, he realized, what had been missing when he was growing up. The ability to choose.

"I'm trying to *give* you the choice," Kennedy insisted. "I'm trying to give you both a choice."

He felt as if she were trying to take it away from him, as if she were trying to take Pru and Ari and the life they'd made off the board as viable options. It just made him want to hold on tighter. "Even if I wasn't comin' to realize that keepin' an inn is just in my blood, your sister's under my skin, and I'd choose her anyway. I'd choose her over anything else."

Kennedy frowned, clearly not sure how to respond. "Flynn, I don't think—"

"No, you're not thinking. Not past the surface. You lived the gypsy life, and you know what it is to come home again. And you also know what it is to have no one believin' in you that you'll stay."

"It's not the same," she insisted.

"Can't you see that it is? I found home with her. With them both. The story of how we met may be lie, but the rest is God's truth, and I'd thank you to have a little goddamn faith—in me and in her."

Kennedy stared at him. "You're in love with her."

"Isn't that what I've been saying?" he demanded. When she only continued to stare, he raked a hand through his hair. "Did that possibility really never occur to you?"

"No."

Flynn scowled at her. "Well, that doesn't reflect particularly well on any of us."

"It's just…I never would have imagined you changing your entire life like this. You love to travel, love to perform."

"So do you," he pointed out. "And you came back."

"That was different. My roots were here. This is you changing literally everything. Because that's what this means. She's not free to pick up and go with you if you get a wild hair."

"I'm not asking her to." He met Kennedy's jewel green eyes. "Look, she's not ready yet to believe that everything between us is real, not ready to believe that I'll really stay. You haven't helped with that by reminding her exactly how many people have broken their word to her."

"I'm just trying to protect her."

"So am I. I love her. She can't accept the words just yet, not without action to back it up. I'm ready and willing to wait her out on that. In the meantime, I made her a promise to stay by her side and see this through. And that's exactly what I intend to do."

"Okay."

It was Flynn's turn to blink. "Okay? That's it?"

"That's it. You're one of my best friends,

Flynn, and one of the best men I know. Do you really think I'm going to object to the idea of having you as a brother-in-law?"

"So you're okay with this? With us?"

"I want her happy. And despite the strange circumstances you're in, I can see that you make her happy. But…"

"Of course, there's a but." This conversation had gone far too well.

"Have a care. She's never let any other man get this close. You have noble intentions, but you're in a position to hurt her worse than anyone else ever has."

"Hurting her is the last thing, I'd ever want to do."

"Let's just hope that's a promise you're able to keep."

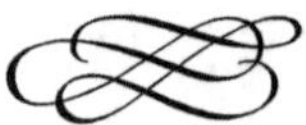

CHAPTER 12

"I CAN'T BELIEVE MAGGIE agreed that easily." Pru stared at the laptop, as if her sister was going to put through another Skype call to say she'd changed her mind. She'd gone into the family meeting prepared for a fight and instead she'd gotten full support.

Athena spoke from the laptop, where she'd yet to sign off the call. "She's still so thrown by your engagement, I think she's happy to see evidence that you're still sane. Business makes sense to her, so don't look a gift horse in the mouth."

As Pru absorbed the reminder of her recklessness, Kennedy wrapped an arm around her shoulders. "The spa is a great idea, and the business plan supports that. After all the work we put into that thing the last two weeks, I'd have been shocked if she said anything but yes."

"It didn't hurt that Porter is basically volunteering himself and whichever ones of us he can corral as free labor on his days off to get started on what can be done without a full crew," Xander added, giving Porter the side eye.

Porter just grinned. "C'mon, Xan, when was the last time we swung a hammer together?"

"Without being paid for it? That would be the old treehouse, when we were thirteen. Building stuff is your first love, not mine."

"I'm sure your wife will see that you're fairly compensated for the time." Porter punctuated the statement with an eyebrow waggle.

"Teenager present!" Pru warned.

"It's cute how you think that should bother me," Ari said.

Xander scrubbed a hand over his face. "God save us when you start dating."

"That won't be until she's thirty," Flynn insisted. He said it so easily, as if there was no question he'd be here when Ari turned thirty.

Hugging the idea of it to her heart, Pru declared, "I'm on board with this plan." She already had so many things to worry about with acquiring a teenager. Adding dating to the mix just seemed like borrowing trouble.

Ari made a big, dramatic show of rolling her eyes, but Pru caught the smile. She liked being the center of everyone's attention. At least there was no question that she was loved.

"Do you have your stuff packed?" Kennedy asked her.

"Already in the foyer."

"Then let's roll. There's a pizza at the tavern with our name on it."

"Pizza is an entirely appropriate celebration for such a momentous occasion as opening a spa," Flynn declared. "Particularly in lieu of an adult beverage. Raise a slice for me."

"We just had supper two hours ago," Pru protested.

"That was supper. This is dinner," Ari explained, grabbing the last clementine from the bowl on the counter. "Did you miss the part where I turned into a hobbit this summer?"

"A hobbit who's been eating her body weight in clementines."

Ari shrugged and popped a wedge of fruit into her mouth. "At least I won't get scurvy."

"That you won't. Have fun at your sleepover."

"I'm gonna trounce Kennedy at *Killer Bunnies*."

Kennedy went brows up. "Should I be afraid?"

"Beware the Cyberbunny," Flynn intoned. *Killer Bunnies* was another of Ari's favorite board games that she'd introduced Flynn to through a sound thrashing.

"Noted. Come on Xander. Let's roll."

In a noisy knot, they all headed for the front door. Ari paused to give Flynn a tight hug. After an instant of hesitation, he squeezed her back, an expression of stunned pleasure on his face that had Pru's heart melting. He stroked a hand over Ari's ponytail. "Have fun, *cailín beag.*"

"Oh, I will." She moved to Pru, offering a fast, hard squeeze. "Night, Mom."

Pru's heart stumbled. "Night, baby."

Ari scooped up her backpack, and on a wink whispered, "Enjoy the empty house. I'm sure you'll find an appropriate means of celebrating." Then she shut the door smartly behind her.

"Did she just…" Pru began.

"I do believe she did," Flynn confirmed. "Don't think about it too hard. Your head might explode." He wrapped his arms around her. "And how are you feeling about that little display there, Mum?"

Pru sighed and snuggled in. "I need a minute. My heart's rolled over to show its soft underbelly."

Flynn rested his cheek on the top of her

head. "Mine, too. She's an incredibly appealing kid."

"She likes having a big messy family around, as unconventional as this one may be."

"It's a great family. Even if Xander keeps giving me those 'I have a badge and I will use it against you, if necessary' looks."

She pulled back to look up at him. "He's not hassling you, is he?"

"No. He's worried about the circumstances, which we all are. I don't blame him for it. He knows me the least, so it's natural he'd be concerned. I'd think less of him if he didn't look out for you."

"Xander's never been easy with lies or secrets." Neither had she. But in this case, the ends justified the means. "Either way, it seems like you and Kennedy are back on reasonable footing."

"We've sorted things out. Enough about your family for now. We do, in fact, have an empty house and no guests expected until tomorrow. What do we want to do with it?"

A smile tugged at Pru's mouth. "I expect you have some ideas."

"It happens that I do. Go get on some shoes you can walk in and grab a couple of towels."

She blinked. "Shoes? Towels?"

"We've no one to look after here, and it's after dark. I think it's high time we revisited Opal Springs and pick up where we were so rudely interrupted after Kennedy's wedding."

"Oh!" Heat sparked low in her belly. "Well, okay then."

By the time she came back with the requested towels, he was waiting by the back door, a picnic basket and blanket in hand.

"You've thought this out."

"I have. I've thought a lot of things out about tonight. C'mon."

With that cryptic statement, he took her hand and they made their way by flashlight down the trail. Opal Springs was much as it had been more than a month before, except there was no echo of a party, no sign of other people who stood to interrupt. They were completely, wonderfully alone, with nothing but a symphony of crickets for company. Now that the sun was down, the heat of the day was fading.

Flynn spread out the blanket on the bank and opened the basket.

"Champagne?" Pru asked. "Are we celebrating something?"

"I hope we will be."

What does that mean? she wondered.

Instead of opening it immediately, he nestled the bottle in a notch of the rocks, submerged in the cool water, setting a pair of glasses on the bank above. Then he pulled off his shirt and Pru was distracted from anything else but the way his bare chest gleamed in the moonlight. A dusting of dark hair narrowed to a trail that disappeared into the waistband of the jeans he'd already unbuttoned. She itched to touch, to feel the warmth of his skin beneath her palms, against her own bare flesh.

Flynn caught her looking and grinned.

"You're looking at me like I'm an ice cream sundae on the hottest day of summer."

"Well, now you're just making me think about licking chocolate sauce off your abs."

"We'll add it to the list."

Pru reached for her own shirt, tugging it up and off. "We have a list?"

"To be sure. I've been adding to it by the day. But you started it here, that night of Kennedy's wedding, with the invitation to go skinny dipping. Why was that?"

"Here in particular or with you?"

"Well, I hope it was with me because you couldn't resist my roguish charm." As he spoke, Flynn shucked his jeans and Pru got a very clear view of his…charm.

"Um." What were they talking about?

He laughed and jumped into the water. A moment later, he surfaced, black hair slicked back like a seal. "So, really, why skinny dipping?"

"Oh." She stripped out of the rest of her own

clothes. "Because I'd never done it before. Never even thought of doing it. It always seemed reckless, and I don't do reckless. I don't know when that started to bother me."

She leapt, splashing into the spring and losing her breath. Compared to the warm night air, the water closing over her head was one step above frigid. She broke the surface on a gasp. "Holy crap, this is so much colder at night!"

Flynn swam the few feet over and snagged her around the waist, hauling her back against his body. "So, you thought you'd be a little reckless. And how does it feel now?"

Her back pressed to his chest, and his hands splayed across her belly, holding her in place and relieving her of the need to do much more than kick a little to stay afloat. She tipped her head back against his shoulder, looking past the canopy of trees up to the star-studded sky. "It feels…decadent. And a little wicked."

He pressed a kiss to her ear and slid one

hand a little further south. "I think we can do better than a little wicked."

"I'm counting on it." She wiggled a little, trying to urge his hand lower.

"But first—" Flynn spun her around in his arms, settling his hands at the small of her back. "—there are things I need to say."

"You sound awfully serious." Pru didn't know what to make of that and resisted the urge to draw back. He wouldn't wait until she was naked and aroused to drop bad news.

"We got into this because we didn't feel we had a choice."

She went stiff, but he held her tight when she would've pulled away.

"We've spent all this time worrying about the lies and the consequences. But the truth is, other than the when and how we met, I haven't lied about anything. I haven't regretted a single moment I've spent with you." He grabbed her left hand and lifted it from the water, bringing it to his lips to kiss the ring he'd put there.

"When I gave you this ring, I asked if you'd wear it and take what comes, with me by your side, partners 'til the end. We had some hazy notion of an end date, sometime after the threat to the adoption was past. But things have changed."

Pru's chest went tight with some strange mix of anxiety and anticipation. "They have?"

He nodded, more serious than she'd ever seen him. "They have. I'm in love with you."

The admission stole her breath, had her hands digging into his shoulders.

"I think I was more than half there when I bought this ring. I want to stay, not just for cover, but for real. I want to make a family with you and Ari. And I want to ask you again, if you'll keep wearing my ring and take what comes, with me by your side, partners 'til death do we part? Will you marry me, Pru?"

Her heart was going to beat straight out of her chest. Emotion lodged a hard fist in her throat. She wanted what he offered. Wanted it with a bone-deep desperation she'd never known. And yet…"What about your travels? Your music? The whole vagabond lifestyle? I can't do that. I'm tied here."

"My music's a part of me, and I'll play no matter where I am. As to the rest, I left home as a boy, and I've had my adventures, seen much of the world. I'm a man grown now, and I want home. For me, that's you. And you're here, so I want to stay. Will you have me?"

I want to stay. The four most beautiful words she'd ever heard. The words no one else had ever given her.

Eyes brimming, she framed his face. "I could never ask you to stay. You had to choose it on your own."

He pressed his brow to hers. "I did. I do. I choose you."

You're here, so I want to stay. I choose you.

Finally. After all these years, all this time and effort taking care of everyone else, he was the one taking care of her. And she could let him because he'd chosen her. He loved her enough to stay. "I love you. God, how I love you."

"Is that a yes?"

Pru laughed through the sheen of tears. "Yes. Yes, I'll marry you."

"Then I'd say now we can celebrate."

AFTER NEARLY FIFTEEN years of avoiding anything resembling routine, Flynn found himself settling into one with an ease he wouldn't have imagined. Guests came and went, and he didn't feel a flicker of the envy that had plagued him as a child. He enjoyed meeting and chatting with each one, and finding a way to personalize their visit. Most swore they'd come back, and that gave him a sense of pride he hadn't felt working his parents' B and B. Here he was contributing to what Pru and her sisters were building, making it grow and thrive. And he was putting down roots for the first time in his adult life, twined around the woman he loved and the girl who'd already become a daughter in his heart. Life was good, and he could *almost* forget the threat hanging over their heads.

Almost.

Then Lydia Coogan called, requesting a meeting with him and Pru, and all his newly engaged bliss was eradicated in a twist of anxiety. This woman could destroy everything.

"What do you suppose she wants?" Flynn asked.

"She said she needed some clarification on a few things in your application." Pru laid a hand on his arm. "I'm sure it's fine. We went back and forth with Mae a few times, getting all the details right, and she'd known us most of our lives. It's not surprising she needs some more information."

"What if we're asked to produce documentation of our relationship? Emails or whatever?"

"I don't think they can do that. They aren't immigration." But now she looked as worried as he felt.

Immigration. There was another bridge they'd have to cross. But one thing at a time.

Flynn slipped his arms around her. "I'm sorry. I didn't mean to add to your stress. I'm just nervy is all."

She burrowed in. "I'm ready for all of this to be settled, so it's not hanging over our heads."

"Your mouth to God's ear. Where's Ari?"

"Upstairs trying on every article of clothing she owns, trying to decide on a first day of school outfit. I can't believe summer's nearly over."

"You've had lots of changes."

"This year has been…crazy. I lost my mother, got Kennedy back, gained a daughter, started a new business, and found you. I barely recognize my life anymore."

Flynn laced his fingers at her back. "A lot of good in there, though."

"Yeah." She lifted her head. "I wish my mother could've met you."

It wasn't lost on Flynn that had Joan still been alive, he might never have stuck around long enough to get here. Would Pru have made that first move without the impending adoption hanging over her head? Would he have even realized what he was missing? "I wish I could've met her. I heard so many stories about her over the years. Kennedy loved her very much."

"We all did. She had the biggest heart. Nobody loved like she did."

He stroked a hand through her hair. "I'd say the apple didn't fall far from the tree."

Her lips curved. The knock on the door wiped the smile right off her face. "Oh sure, now she knocks," Pru muttered.

"Friendly, professional," Flynn murmured. "We've got this." He hoped he was right.

Pru had a welcoming smile pasted on as she opened the door. "Miss Coogan. Welcome. Please come in."

As before, Lydia Coogan was dressed in business attire, the briefcase slung over her shoulder. Her no nonsense shoes tapped an impatient rhythm as she strode inside.

"Can I offer you some coffee? A glass of tea?"

"No." After an absurdly long pause, she added. "Thank you."

Pru's smile flickered. "All right then. Please come through to the family parlor. We won't be disturbed there."

The woman perched on the edge of one of the chairs, back ramrod straight. Flynn and Pru sat across from her on the sofa. There'd be no relaxing during this meeting, and maybe there shouldn't be. This woman had set herself up as enemy from day one. He reached automatically for Pru's hand, feeling a matching tension coiling through her.

"I'll be brief," Miss Coogan said.

Flynn doubted she knew how to be anything but.

She pulled a file out of the briefcase, flipping it open. "I've been checking your references, Mr. Bohannon. The six you provided all checked out, though all expressed their surprise at your involvement with Miss Reynolds."

"As we said before, we kept our relationship quiet," Flynn said.

Miss Coogan ignored that. "I'm sure you read in the paperwork, each of your references is then asked to provide an additional reference as part of the process. I've been working my way through those, which has taken some time, given the time difference between here and Ireland."

Was he supposed to apologize for that?

She consulted something in the file. "Miss Reynolds, you arrived in Galway on May twenty-fifth, two years ago, correct?"

"Yes."

"You and your sister Kennedy spent a day there, before traveling to Ennis, where you met Mr. Bohannon."

"That's correct."

"Where did you meet him?"

"He was playing in a pub there."

Miss Coogan's gaze felt almost hostile as she flicked it from Pru back to the notes in her lap. "And do either of you happen to remember the name of that pub?"

"No. Callahan's? Gallagher's? One of those Irish surnames probably. I was there for two weeks, and I ate in a lot of pubs. I don't remember that one in particular. Certainly not after all this time."

"What about you, Mr. Bohannon?" Flynn wasn't mistaking the harsh gleam in her eye as she stared him down.

"I've played in literally hundreds of pubs over my career. I could name half a dozen pubs I've played in Ennis over the years, but I couldn't tell you which one I played that night."

The woman nodded, as if that confirmed something. "Understandable. Since you weren't in Ennis at all."

Ice crawled up Flynn's spine, and Pru's hand flexed in his. "Excuse me?"

"You were not in Ennis at the time Pru and Kennedy Reynolds were going through. You weren't even in Ireland. See, one of your references put me in touch with one Darcy O'Hara. He said if anyone knew anything about you being involved with a woman, it would be her."

Oh fuck.

Pru frowned. "Who is Darcy O'Hara?"

But it was Lydia Coogan who answered. "One of his groupies, apparently. She followed him on the road for nearly a year, trailing him from venue to venue. During the period in question, she—and he—were in Paris, playing Corcoran's Irish Pub. She emailed me very detailed notes on the itinerary, including pictures and plane tickets that prove that you could not possibly have crossed paths with Miss Reynolds on that trip."

Pru opened her mouth, then closed it again.

Flynn felt the ice turn to sweat. "Darcy was more or less a stalker. She could have invented any number of things, and likely would once she heard I was getting married."

"Perhaps she could. But she didn't. You lied, Mr. Bohannon. Both of you lied." She expanded her gimlet stare to include Pru. "And your sister and her husband are complicit."

Pru's face had gone white. "I can explain."

Miss Coogan slammed the file shut and shoved it into her briefcase. "I don't care, Miss Reynolds. I didn't like this situation from the beginning. I don't appreciate bending of the rules to accommodate people. The rules exist for a reason. But if you think I'm going to allow Ari Rosas to stay in your care, you have another thing coming. I'm pursuing an injunction to have her removed from the home."

"No! You can't!" Pru was on her feet in a second.

The social worker slammed the briefcase shut. "I can and I will. Liars have no business raising a child. I don't know what game you're playing, but it will be over by the end of the week, I can assure you."

"We'll fight you on this," Flynn snarled. He had no idea how, but there had to be something.

Coogan flashed a humorless smile. "Go ahead and try."

Pru followed as the woman headed for the front door. "Miss Coogan, please. Just listen."

"The time for listening is past. The time for truth is past. I suggest you start saying your goodbyes."

The house shook as she shut the door behind her.

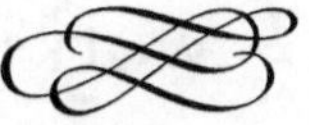

PRU FLATTENED HER PALMS against the door, shock and denial arcing through her. No. No, this couldn't be happening. She'd done everything right. She'd taken the classes, gotten the certifications, and picked up her mother's mantle without complaint. She'd been a goddamned rock since her mother died—for Ari and her sisters, because they needed her to be. Surely, all of that would outweigh her one indiscretion.

A car cranked up outside. Pru's knees gave out, and she collapsed like a puppet with cut strings. Flynn caught her before she hit the floor. His arms came tight around her. He was saying something. She didn't know if it was English or Gaelic. Her ears weren't working. Her legs weren't working. Nothing was working in the face of the tearing grief. Nothing could touch the unspeakable horror of what had just happened. She curled in on herself, wrapping both arms around her middle, as if that could contain the horrific pain. Tears poured down her cheeks and she opened her mouth, but nothing came out. Her entire body felt like a scream that couldn't escape.

She was going to lose Ari. She was going to lose the last piece of her mother. Her family would never trust her again. And she was letting down the child, who was counting on her more than anyone else in the world. The child she'd sworn to protect and love all of her days. After a lifetime of playing it safe, one reckless decision had destroyed it all.

It broke her. More than being abandoned by her father. More than the death of her mother.

The realization that she'd done this, she'd made this mistake, shattered her. All the agony she'd repressed and ignored for years came flooding out in a silent storm.

Flynn held her as she shook and sobbed. A part of her wanted to shove him away. A part wished she'd never seen him, never met him, never been tempted by him. But that put the responsibility off on someone else, and it had been her decision. Her foolish wish. This disaster wasn't on him. Pushing him away wouldn't change anything, and she had sufficient wits remaining to realize that, when all this was over, he was the only one likely to still stand by her. That thought had her turning into him at last, fisting her hands in his shirt and tucking into his body.

An eon later, the tears finally slowed, probably because she'd wept out every drop of moisture in her body. Pru's head throbbed. Not for the first time, she thought grief felt much like the flu—an attack on all the senses that left you weak and aching. Flynn's hand was tangled in her hair, stroking her nape. He'd stopped speaking at some point. They were still in the floor of the foyer. Pru felt some dim measure of gratitude for the fact that no guests had stumbled upon them. But they couldn't stay here.

She lifted her head to find Flynn's eyes red-rimmed.

"I'm sorry," he choked out. "I'm so fucking sorry."

Pru tried to shake her head, but it weighed a thousand pounds. "Not your fault."

"But if I—"

"It doesn't matter. What's done is done. And we have to face the consequences." The social worker would carry through on her threat, and a judge could rule to take Ari away. Nothing could be worse than that, and she'd have to find a way to live with it. They all would.

"There has to be something we can do."

She crawled out of his lap, using the door-knob to haul herself to her feet. Purged of that first wave of grief, she struggled to focus on practical steps, on action. "I need to call Robert."

"Who's Robert?"

"Robert Barth. My attorney. I probably should have done that in the first place, but I knew he'd object to what we were doing, and I was afraid of what he might tell me about the alternatives. He needs to know what's going on. And maybe there's something to be done to fight it."

Feeling about a hundred years old, Pru made her way to the kitchen, pouring a tall glass of water she didn't want and guzzling it down. Then she poured a second to chase some ibuprofen. "I should call Mae, too. She's still on leave and recovering from back surgery, but maybe she can offer some insight. Or maybe she can talk Lydia Coogan down." Not that she had much faith in that eventuality. The woman had taken an instant dislike to Pru and seemed determined to punish her for being able to get past any of the red tape of the foster system.

"We have to tell the rest of the family that

this is coming." The idea of having to face that made her want to run. Or maybe just hide in a closet.

Flynn's expression was grim. "We'll do it together."

That didn't make her feel better, exactly, but she felt a little less alone.

"I have to talk to Ari."

"Do you want to speak to the attorney first? Find out more information?"

Pru shook her head. "There's nothing worse as a foster kid than to have adults making decisions about you without including you. It's why she eavesdrops. We all did it. I don't want her drawing her own conclusions based on partial information. I have to be honest with her." She set the glass aside and started for the stairs.

"What? Now?"

"The sooner the better. We don't know if she came downstairs at any point. I don't think she overheard the social worker or she'd have been up in the middle of that meeting arguing. But if she saw us in the foyer... She needs to know where she stands. I've never lied to her, and I'm not going to start now."

He started after her.

"I think, maybe, I need to have this conversation with her alone."

Flynn pulled up short. After a moment's hesitation, he nodded. "I'm right here if either of you need me."

"Thank you." Because they both needed it, Pru laid a hand against his cheek before going upstairs.

Dread ratcheted higher with each step. She tried to find the words, the right thing to say so that this didn't destroy Ari's world, but her mind was simply full of static. Too late, it occurred to her that she should probably wash her face. But no amount of scrubbing was going to cover up the crying, so ultimately, she knocked on Ari's door.

No answer.

Maybe she'd fallen asleep?

Pru knocked again, twisting the knob and pushing the door open. "Ari? Honey?"

Her room looked like a bomb had gone off. Clothes were scattered on every surface. Good lord, they needed to have a chat about the importance of everything in its place. She didn't realize that she'd expected to see Ari passed out amid the piles until her brain registered that there was no teenager in the room.

"Ari?" She strode to the closet, though the door stood open. Empty.

Pru wandered back into the hall, checking the bathrooms. No Ari. She headed upstairs. When guests weren't in residence, sometimes Ari liked to read in the turret room. But that, too, was empty. She trotted back to the landing.

"Flynn, can you run look to see if Ari's outside or in the barn?"

"Sure."

As the door shut behind him, she began going room-by-room, including the guest rooms. Unease morphed into active worry when she found no trace of her child. Where was she? Kennedy's old room was the last one, and again, no Ari. Pru started to shut the door, when she caught a flash of movement. The curtain billowed from a breeze coming in the open window. The window that opened on to the old bodock tree. The one Kennedy had used for sneaking out to meet Xander.

Everybody knew that story, including Ari.

Flynn came up the stairs. "I didn't find her." He looked past her. "Why is the window open?"

Pru couldn't breathe.

Ari always eavesdropped. If she'd heard what the social worker had said, if she'd heard that she'd be taken away…she might run. It was that fear that had driven Pru and her sisters to fight so hard for Ari to stay put after their mother died. Kennedy had stated unequivocally that running was what she'd have done.

As she stared at the open window, Pru realized that she'd been wrong. The situation could absolutely get worse. "We have to call Xander. I think Ari's run away."

"WE CAN'T FIND HER." Pru's voice, already ragged from crying, broke again as she met Xander on the porch. The sound of it shredded Flynn's guts. This was his fault. If he hadn't opened his big fat mouth… If he hadn't convinced Pru that this was the best course of action… If he'd never stayed at all, this never would have happened. Ari's home wouldn't have been at risk.

Xander put an arm around her. "We're gonna find her. I promise. Let's go inside now. I need to get some more information." He turned to the deputy he'd brought with him. "Clyde, you wanna do a sweep of the immediate area, see what you can find?"

"Yes, sir."

"We've shouted ourselves hoarse, and we've searched the house and barn," Flynn said, barely trusting his own voice.

"Won't hurt to have another pair of eyes," Xander said easily.

He escorted them to the kitchen and put on

the kettle himself. "You sit on down. I'm gonna make you some tea."

Tea. Flynn should have thought of that. Pru's throat was raw. It would do her good if they could get it down her.

"When did you last see Ari?" Xander asked.

Pru scooped a hand through her hair. "I… about an hour and a half ago? Maybe two hours? She was trying to pick an outfit for the first day of school. I went up to talk to her about half an hour ago, but she wasn't in her room or anywhere else in the house, and the window in Kennedy's room was open to the old bodock. You know how much she glommed onto that story of Kennedy using it to sneak out."

"That she did. Did she take her phone?"

"It's still on her dresser," Pru said.

Kennedy burst into the room. "I came as soon as I could." She wrapped her arms around her sister. "What happened?"

"We were just getting to that," Xander said.

"Why do you think she ran away as opposed just going off hiking without telling you?"

"She's always really good about asking permission for things," Pru said.

"Her backpack is gone," Flynn added. "Along with the entire bag of clementines, a box of granola bars, and part of the new case of bottled water."

"You're sure that's not just up in her room?" Kennedy asked. "Foster kids often hoard food. I've never known Ari to do that, but you never know."

"I—" Pru paused. "I don't know. We didn't check. Her room looks like a bomb went off."

"Ransacked?" Xander's voice sharpened.

"Teenage girl," Pru corrected. "She wasn't taken. She ran."

"Why would she run?" Kennedy asked.

Pru closed her eyes, her face twisting in pain, and the guilt nearly buckled Flynn's knees.

He laid a hand on her shoulder, almost surprised when Pru's hand came up to cover his. "Lydia Coogan was here."

The tension in the room ratcheted up exponentially. For the first time in their long friendship, Flynn saw an ugly suspicion darken Kennedy's gaze as she stared him down, waiting for the explanation he'd give almost anything not to tell.

"She knows that we lied, and she's planning to seek an injunction to have Ari removed from the house."

Xander swore, low and vicious.

"How?" Kennedy demanded. "How could she possibly find out? I covered for you."

"Someone pointed her to Darcy."

"Oh shit. Because your stalker is the best character reference for an adoption."

"I don't know who thought she'd be a good reference. Either way, she had proof I wasn't in Ireland when Pru was."

Xander folded his massive arms, his gray eyes cold. "I told you. I told you both this was a bad idea."

Flynn's temper spiked. Recriminations helped absolutely nothing. They were wasting time. Ari was out there somewhere, on her own. "You feel free to kick my ass six ways from Sunday as soon as this is all over. I guarantee you absolutely nothing you can say or do is worse than what I'm saying to myself. But right now, Ari's out there, on her own, thinking God knows what. I don't matter. She does."

Kennedy put a restraining hand on Xander's arm. "This woman said that in front of Ari? That she was going to take her away?"

Pru shook her head. "No. But you know how she eavesdrops. If she heard that…"

"She'd run," Kennedy concurred. "It's what I'd have done. Leave on my own terms. It's what I did do before I came to Mom."

Clyde knocked on the back door. At Xander's gesture, he came on into the kitchen. "I didn't find any sign, Sheriff."

Xander inhaled a slow breath and scrubbed both hands over his face. "All right. What was she wearing?"

"I don't know if she left in the same thing she had on earlier," Pru said.

"What was that?"

"Blue jean shorts. That Volunteers t-shirt Logan brought her, I think. But she'd been changing outfits."

"Run up to her room and see if you can sort out whether that's there," Xander ordered.

"I'll go with you," Kennedy said.

When they'd left the room, he pulled out his cell phone and dialed. "Essie, I need you to put out an immediate BOLO statewide for Ariana Rosas. Hispanic female, aged thirteen, approximately 5'3", 110 pounds. Black hair down to her shoulder blades, brown eyes. Runaway. I—Yes, I know, Essie. That's not pertinent to this BOLO. She was last seen wearing denim shorts and a UT Volunteers t-shirt—orange with white text. She has, at most, a two-hour head start. Probably less. She's believed to have a backpack with her."

"It's blue," Flynn offered, feeling sick as Xander nodded and continued.

"We're going to do a broader sweep here, then I'll get the release signed to put her into NCIC. This close to the state line, she could hit North Carolina, Virginia, or Kentucky, if she managed to hitchhike."

Hitchhiking. Mary, Mother of God. Flynn hadn't thought he could feel sicker than he already did. What kind of lunatic might she encounter if she tried to do that? She could get hurt. Or worse. Feeling absolutely useless and twitching with the need to move, he curled his hands to fists.

Xander talked a few more minutes, giving instructions regarding the mobilization of resources, as he finished making the tea he'd started. "Do you know if Chris is in town? No, no, I'll call her myself." He hung up the phone and gave Flynn a long, indecipherable look.

What could Flynn say? *I'm sorry* was paltry and wholly inadequate. *I'm sorry* didn't undo any of this. He had no excuse, no justification. Under the circumstances, the fact that he loved Pru and Ari both meant nothing. He'd stayed intending to make their lives better, not cause them more pain.

"We're going to find her." Xander's tone was hard. So was his expression. But Flynn took some comfort in the other man's conviction. Xander loved this child, too, and he wouldn't rest until she was home. For however much longer that lasted.

They both looked up as Pru and Kennedy came back into the room.

"The UT t-shirt isn't in her room, and it looks like maybe she took a few other jeans and t-shirts, along with one of her hoodies. And her piggy bank was empty," Pru reported.

"The food and water weren't up there, so it looks like she took those with her," Kennedy added.

"That's good. We don't have immediate concerns about dehydration. You said she left her phone. Any other electronic devices?" Xander asked.

"No. We'd been talking about getting her a Kindle with all the Percy Jackson books for her birthday, but that's not for another three months." Pru knit her hands.

"That's fine. Cell reception is often spotty up here anyway. Is she on social media?"

A brief look of horror crossed her face. "I… don't know. That's a thing a parent should know." Her voice shot up half an octave.

"Kacy would probably know if she were," Flynn said.

"I'll call and get up with her mom," Kennedy said. She gave Pru's arm a squeeze before walking out of the room.

"Okay. It's okay. Now I've got to make some more phone calls, get some things organized. You're gonna sit right down here and drink your tea." Xander brought a mug over to the table.

"I don't want tea," she snapped. "I want my daughter!"

"I know it. But you're gonna need your voice to call for her when we get out searching here in a little bit. So drink your tea and soothe your throat."

She looked so brittle, Flynn was afraid to touch her, even in comfort. But she sat and began to sip at the tea. He parked himself at the kitchen window, watching the yard so he didn't say something to make the whole situation worse. Within half an hour, the drive was as full of vehicles as it normally was for one of their Friday night jam sessions. But there was no celebratory air here. Flynn's heart squeezed as he recognized Porter and Logan; Kennedy's boss, Denver; Ford McIntosh, and half a dozen other friends he'd made through his time here. Some kind of command center was being set up on the porch.

"Glad you could make it." Xander's voice brought Flynn around to see a woman and a dog standing in the kitchen doorway.

The woman crossed to him, offering her hand. "Of course. I'm just relieved I was in town."

"Chris, this is my sister-in-law, Pru and her fiancé, Flynn Bohannon."

Chris nodded and shook Pru's hand, as

Xander continued introductions. "This is Chris Sargent and Dash, from the Stone County Search and Rescue team. They're going to help us figure out which way to look."

"Search and rescue?" Pru's face went impossibly paler. "I thought they only came out for extreme circumstances."

"Normally yes, but I happened to be in town, and I'm happy to help," Chris said easily. "I'll need you to find something Ari has worn recently that hasn't been washed. Dirty socks or pajamas. Something she'd have worn close to the skin."

This Flynn could handle. "She brought laundry down this morning. I don't think it got started yet." He bolted for the laundry room and dug through her hamper. Thank God, they'd started on guest sheets first. Back in the kitchen he held out the white, pink, and gold fabric with *Princess of Sassytown* printed on the side. "They're the socks she wore horseback riding the other day."

"Good. That's great. It'll be exactly what we

need." The dog sitting beside her practically vibrated with bright-eyed excitement, but he didn't move other than to look to Chris for orders. "Dash will use this to catch Ari's scent and will figure out which way she went. As she lives here and has spent a lot of time around the yard, he may criss-cross a bit, but we'll find her trail. Just be patient."

"Go do your thing. Thanks for coming, Chris," Xander said.

The woman nodded, then she and Dash headed outside.

"What do we do in the meantime?" Flynn demanded.

"You get prepped for a hike. Proper boots and packs. We don't know how long we'll be out."

But Flynn knew. He'd stay out as long as it took.

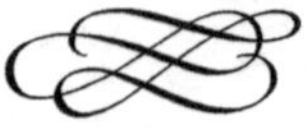

CHAPTER 14

THE SUN SLID BEHIND the ridge that gave the town its name, and Pru knew full dark wasn't far behind. "Ari!"

She heard the faint echo of the call from half a dozen other voices spread out across their sector. Her feet ached and exhaustion dragged at her frame, but she kept going. She'd keep going until she held Ari in her arms again. An hour before, Dash had found the peel from a clementine—the first and only proof Ari had actually headed out cross country instead of going for the road. The only comfort there was that they didn't have the danger of some human predator picking her up trying to hitchhike. One thirteen-year-old girl couldn't cover that much territory in six hours, so she had to be in the geographic area. But on foot, with night falling, the mountains Pru had run tame in as a child felt like a whole other country.

Was Ari scared? Her trail had led them in a southerly direction, skirting town. Where was she going? Did she even have a plan? How much of one could she really have come up with in the half hour she had to slip out of the house? She was resourceful, but she hadn't had the same kind of hard life before coming to Joan that many fosters had. She hadn't had to learn to survive. Certainly not any kind of wilderness survival.

"Ari!" Flynn's voice carried from somewhere up ahead. She could barely see him in the dimming light.

"He's not handling this well," Kennedy murmured.

"No." Pru had watched him retreat over the

course of the day, and she hadn't been able to do anything about it. No amount of comforting was going to help him until they had Ari back. And then there'd be a showdown with a judge. "He blames himself."

"Do you?"

Pru looked to her sister, wondering if *she* blamed her friend. "No, not at all. I agreed to all of this. If anyone's to blame, it's me for wanting one last thing for me before the adoption." She looked back to the trail. "I feel like I'm being punished." And didn't she deserve that for being so selfish?

Kennedy stopped in her tracks, reaching out to grab her by the arm. "Pru." Absolute horror was etched on her face. "No one expected you to stop living your own life when you decided to adopt Ari. Of course, you deserve someone."

She'd believed she did deserve someone. It was the thing that had pushed her so far out of character as to pursue Flynn. "But at this cost?" She'd been thinking about it all afternoon as they searched, between bouts of panic over whether her child was safe. No amount of logic would change the fact that, if she hadn't broken out of the pigeon hole everyone kept her in, none of this would have happened. "If anything's happened to her, I'll never forgive myself."

"We're going to find her, and she's going to be *fine*." Kennedy's voice held a savage edge, as if daring the Universe to contradict her.

"And the rest?" Finding her didn't mean they got to keep her. And because of their deception and Kennedy's collusion, it wasn't as if Lydia Coogan would look at *any* member of their family as an option.

"We'll deal with the rest as it comes. As a family. A united front."

Pru didn't know if that would be enough.

One problem at a time. It was how she'd gotten through her mother's death. Compartmentalizing. Facing only what was right in front of her. Right now, that was simply getting through however many hours passed until they found her daughter.

Up ahead, Chris paused and pulled a bowl and water from her pack, pouring some for Dash. The dog eagerly lapped it up. He'd worked as tirelessly as the rest of them.

Kennedy pulled water from her own pack and shoved it at Pru. "Here. Drink."

Pru didn't argue, gulping it down. She didn't dare sit. If she sat, her muscles would seize up. She was that kind of tired.

Xander appeared out of the woods, conferring with Chris in a tone too low for Pru to hear. She asked him something, and when he shook his head, she pulled out another flag, this one a neon green instead of the orange she'd been using for the points where Dash had alerted.

"Something's up," Pru said, already heading toward them when Xander broke away. She didn't like the look on his face.

"How are you holding up?"

"I'm fine." She'd have said the same through injury or illness, just to keep searching.

"Night's falling. We have to pull everybody in until morning."

Panic reached up to claw at her throat. "We have flashlights," she insisted. "You said the volunteer fire department had those big search lights."

"They're vehicle mounted, and we can't get vehicles down here. It's not safe for everybody else to be out here after dark."

"We're just going to leave the defenseless child out here on her own?" Flynn demanded. "Fuck that."

"I understand your frustration. I don't want to go in either. But blundering around in the dark is more likely to lead to injury and muck up any trail she's left. There's no sign she's hurt, and she's smart enough to find somewhere to stop for the night. There's no rain in the forecast, and this late in the summer, there's no concern about hypothermia from exposure. We'll be back out at first light, with more people to search for a broader range."

"I'm not going back," Pru said.

Xander's expression shifted to one that clearly said *be reasonable.* "Pru—"

"If you're going to make me stop searching for the night, fine. I'll camp out here. I don't want to waste time having to get all this way in the morning. You said yourself, we can't get vehicles out here."

"You're not packed to camp," he pointed out.

"Neither is she. My daughter is about to be spending the night on the mountain, alone, in the dark. She's going to be terrified. I'm not going back, Xander."

He looked to Flynn, who crossed his arms with a belligerent scowl. "I'm staying, too."

"I'm packed for overnight," Chris said. "Though I don't have enough gear for multiple people."

Xander divided a look between them. "I let you stay out here, you *stay put.* I don't want this to turn into multiple missing persons."

"We won't be stupid," Pru promised.

"I'll have some gear and supplies brought out. We can get a four-wheeler down here."

It took an hour, by which time Chris had her little one-person tent set up and Dash fed. Xander's deputy, Clyde Parker, was the one who came with camping gear.

"Where's Xander?" Pru asked.

"He's coordinating with the rest of the search team, making a plan for tomorrow." Clyde swung off the ATV and unhooked the elastic net holding on his cargo. "Got a couple tents, sleeping bags, and food. Crystal's taken over your kitchen back at the inn and is feeding everybody."

"That's kind of her."

"She sent provisions. There's an active burn ban, so no fire, but we won't go hungry." He hefted one of two coolers off the back.

"We?" Flynn asked.

"I'm camping out here tonight with y'all."

"To make sure we behave and don't keep searching?" Pru asked.

"That and to make sure somebody with some more training is on hand, in case any-thing happens," he said easily. "Your sisters are en route and should be here sometime tomorrow morning. Kennedy stayed back to talk to them. But she sent this." Clyde lifted Flynn's fiddle case. "She thought you might want it."

After a moment's hesitation, Flynn took it.

They set up their minimalist camp. She and Flynn were sharing a tent and a double sleeping bag. Some thoughtful person had made sure they had air pads so they weren't sleeping directly on the hard ground. Crystal had packed fried chicken, macaroni and cheese, and peach cobbler. Thanks to the cooler and expert packing job, it was all still warm. Though she had no appetite, Pru ate, tasting little, but appreciating the effort that had gone into making sure they were fed something solid.

When the meal was finished, Flynn opened his fiddle case. He ran a hand over the instrument itself.

"I didn't think you'd feel like playing," Pru said softly.

"I don't. But I can't do anything else, and sound carries out here. So maybe she'll hear it and be a little less afraid." He brought the fiddle to his shoulder and drew the bow across its strings.

She didn't recognize the song, but the melancholy melody seemed to reach right into her chest and squeeze her heart. He was playing his grief, much as Ari had done after Joan's death. Tears slipped down her cheeks as she listened, even after he rolled into something more cheerful and lilting. He played for near to an hour, and by the time he put down his bow, tears streaked his face as well.

No one spoke as he put his fiddle away and climbed into the tent. Pru didn't think she could sleep, but she wanted to curl around him and offer whatever comfort she could. They'd been in this together from the beginning. There was no reason that should change now.

She crawled in after him, zipping them into the deceptive privacy of the tent. In the opposite corner, he pulled off his shoes and slipped into the sleeping bag. On her side, Pru did the same. He faced away from her, and she cuddled up against his back, wrapping an arm around his waist. His body stayed stiff. Aching in body and soul, she pressed a kiss to his nape and whispered, "I love you."

Flynn loosed a shuddering breath and curled his hand around the one she pressed to his chest. "I love you, too. Get some sleep, *mo mhuirnín.*"

She didn't think she could, but the moment his body relaxed against hers, she was out like a light.

FLYNN WOKE OFTEN, unused to the raucous sounds of the night creatures. Pru slept the sleep of the utterly exhausted, wrapped around him. How she took comfort in being close to him after everything that had happened, he didn't know. How could she even bear to look at him? She'd trusted him. She and Ari both had, buying into his crazy plan instead of booting him out on his ass. The price for that trust was far too high. That singular thought circled through his head in the long stretch of absolute silence before the dawn. He couldn't settle, but he'd cost Pru enough. He wasn't about to rob her of the oblivion of sleep. So, he didn't move until he heard the telltale zipper of one of their companions coming out of a tent.

"It's morning," he murmured.

With a little groan, Pru tightened her hold, burying her face against his back. He felt the moment she realized and remembered as her body went stiff. She took a long, slow breath and seemed to will herself to relax again.

"Did you sleep?"

"A little. You?"

"More than I expected." She sat up running a hand through her hair and refastening her ponytail.

Chris was watering Dash as they emerged. "Morning."

Clyde clambered out. "Christ, I'd give my eye teeth for coffee."

"No coffee, but there are Cokes still in the cooler."

"That'll do."

They each wandered off to find a private tree. By the time Flynn got back, Chris had already collapsed her tent and was sliding out the poles. He did the same, while Pru pulled out the energy bars sent for their breakfast. They ate and packed up camp quickly. Clyde radioed back to the command center at the house.

Xander came back quickly. "We've got a hundred volunteers waiting for orders. Chris, what's your plan? Over."

"Picking back up where we left off. Based on our position, I suggest splitting the volunteers down the middle and sending half out in an arc, coming at us from the opposite side of the ridge, starting at the highway. Seems unlikely Ari made it past that point yesterday." She gave the coordinates.

"Done. There's a whole other group searching town. I don't think she went that way, but one way or the other, we're gonna find her today. Over."

"Copy. We're headed out." Chris gave the handset back to Clyde and pulled out the zip-top bag holding Ari's socks. She opened the bag and held a sock for Dash to sniff. "This is Ari. Find Ari. Find Ari, Dash."

The dog circled their camp once, twice, three times, before setting off toward the south again. They all fell into step behind him. The path they followed led off the ridge and down toward a stream. They crossed it and followed it for a while. Flynn noted what he presumed were animal trails leading away from it here and there. Some of the tracks belonged to things he didn't want to think about. There were predators in these mountains, and Ari had been alone last night.

"Most people, when they're lost, will take the path of least resistance," Chris explained. "They're tired, often injured. A lot of people will follow water, reasoning that will eventually lead to civilization."

Pru looked around the thick woods. "There's definitely no civilization for miles yet. I'm not even quite sure where we are."

Dash barked twice, his head shooting up and his ears pricking, before he bulleted off through the trees. Flynn didn't stop to think, he just ran. Branches tore at his arms and face, as his long legs ate up the distance. When he broke free, he found Dash circling the base of a tree, rearing up on his hind legs and whining. High above, a platform nestled in the branches. As he neared, he saw the scatter of orange peels on the ground. He leapt for the rudimentary ladder nailed to the tree, already climbing before the others caught up.

"Ari?"

A sleepy voice answered. "Flynn?"

"Ari." He made it to the top of the platform and saw her, sitting up from where she'd obviously been sleeping on her backpack. Her face and clothes were smudged with dirt, and there were scratches along her arms and face, but she was all in one piece. Safe.

Flynn hauled himself onto the platform in time for her to launch herself into his arms. She began to cry, hanging onto him like a limpet. "I've got you, *cailín beag*. I've got you." He wrapped his arms tight around her and rocked, sending up prayers and promises to the Almighty in thanks for her safe deliverance.

"I heard you. Last night, I heard you playing."

"Did you?"

"I wanted to answer back, but I didn't have anything with me, and I climbed up here to keep away from any bears."

"Bears?" he asked sharply. Thank God he hadn't known about those. "Clever girl. What is this thing?"

"A hunter's platform. They hide up here for deer hunting."

"Flynn?" Pru called up.

"She's here. She's safe." He held Ari for just a few moments longer before pulling back. "Here now. Let's go down. Pru's been worried about you."

They climbed down together, Flynn going first in case she was unsteady. At the bottom of the ladder, Ari fell into Pru's embrace and they both burst into tears.

"I'm sorry. I'm so sorry, Mom."

Pru squeezed her tight. "It's okay. I'm not mad, baby. I'm just so glad you're okay."

"But I'm not okay," Ari wailed. "That awful woman said she was going to take me away. I don't wanna go away. I wanna stay with you."

Flynn's throat went tight.

Pru's arms tightened around her. "We're gonna deal with that, and you can bet every single one of us is going to fight. But don't you worry about that right now. Let's just get you home."

The crackle of the radio pulled Flynn's attention from the reunion.

Chris was grinning as she made the call back to the command center. "We've found her. Repeat, we've found her. Ari's coming home."

Now he just had to find a way to make sure she stayed there.

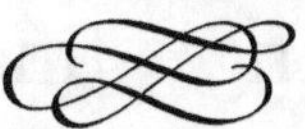

CHAPTER 15

BOTH HIS GIRLS WERE sleeping. Ari looked so small tucked up in their bed, with Pru curled around her. But she was safe. That was the important thing.

Flynn slipped out of the room, quietly shutting the door behind him. The volunteers had been fed and sent home. Someone else had dealt with their two guests, who'd refused to allow their rooms to be comped. Xander was down at the Sheriff's Department, doing whatever it was he did at the end of a search. It was down to family in the house, and that meant it was time for him to face the music.

Pru's sisters were gathered in the family room. They looked up as he strode in.

"They're sleeping, finally." He dropped heavily into a chair himself, as the past twenty-four hours caught up with him.

"You look like you ought to be sleeping, too," Kennedy observed.

"Probably. But there are things to discuss, and I'd as soon do it without Pru. She's been through enough."

Athena poured him two fingers of whiskey from the bottle on the table and walked it over to him. "You're probably gonna need this."

"Thanks." It was barely past noon, but Flynn knocked it back, relishing the way it burned through his exhaustion. Maybe, if he were lucky, it would dull the edge of his guilt.

"Is someone finally going to tell me what's going on?" Maggie demanded.

Flynn had no idea what she'd been told before she flew out, but he didn't see the sense in delaying the inevitable. "Ari ran away because she overheard her social worker telling us yesterday that she's seeking an injunction to have her removed from the home."

"What? Why? What possible justification could they have for that? Pru has been her constant since Mom died. Before that, even."

"Because we got caught in a lie."

"About *what?* Do you have some hideous skeleton in your closet that she uncovered during her background check?"

"No. Not like you're thinking." He eyed the bottle of whiskey and wished for more as fortification for this conversation. "Pru and I didn't meet two years ago in Ireland. We met when I came here for Kennedy's wedding."

Maggie narrowed her eyes. "Why would you lie about that?"

"We were having an affair. Pru's choice. And Ari's new social worker caught us in a position that made our intimate involvement obvious. I knew it would look awful for her to be sleeping with a guest, so I lied and said I was her fiancé.

And as an engagement after less than a week didn't make her look any better, we came up with a different, more plausible backstory."

"So, all of this the past two months has been one big cover up?"

"Yes. And no. I love your sister, and I love Ari. The only thing we lied about is when it started."

"This is…I don't even know what this is." Maggie looked at her sisters. "You knew?"

"I had to sell the cover story," Kennedy said.

"Logan told me they were engaged. I came to get to the bottom of it," Athena said.

"So, I was the only one who didn't know the truth?" The frost in her tone made it clear enough how she felt about that.

"That was my idea," Athena admitted. "None of us were nuts about the deception, but you'd have flipped out worse."

"You're goddamned right I would. And with good reason. How could you endanger Ari like that? How could you not know you'd get caught? What the hell was Pru thinking?"

"That in a lifetime of doing things for everyone else, she'd spend five minutes doing something for herself."

"And look where that got her."

Temper flashed through him, hot and bright as a wildfire. Flynn didn't move, but when he spoke, his voice was iron. "You won't say one word to make her feel more guilt than she already does. She's just been through absolute hell the past twenty-four hours, and there's fresh hell to come because some arrogant, by-the-book woman cares more for her rules than what's in the best interest of that child. You're angry, and justifiably so, but take it out on me. She's been through enough."

He could see a matching flare of temper in Maggie's eyes before she banked it. "I'm not out to berate her. I'm just trying to understand."

How could they not see her as he did?

"All her life, she's been the one you could all count on. Anticipating your needs, cleaning up your messes, being your rock. You're all so used to it, you don't even think about it or consider that she might need or appreciate someone doing the same for her." He'd done that for her. He'd given her the foundation she hadn't even known she'd needed. And it had been one of the most fulfilling things he'd ever done. "She's the most selfless woman I've ever met, and she needs all of you. She'll need you more before all of this is over."

Kennedy frowned. "What are you getting at, Flynn?"

"This is my fault. All of it. And I intend to make that clear to the judge."

"Clear how?" Athena asked.

He gave in to the urge and leaned over to pour himself more whiskey. What did it matter if they judged him now? "I'm going to tell him the truth. I am, apparently, the problem, so if the judge deems it necessary, if he'll let Ari stay with Pru, I'll go." The mere thought was a knife to his gut. To leave the home he'd found here, leave the woman he loved, the child he adored. But what other choice did he have? What other means did he have left to fix what he'd broken?

"You'd walk away from her?" Maggie asked.

Flynn's hand fisted so tight around the glass, he thought it would break. "If I have to."

"She loves you," Kennedy murmured.

"And I love her. But she can eventually get over me. She'll never get over the loss of that child. And there is nowhere on earth better for Ari than with Pru. She's more important than I am. It's what she needs. So, if the judge will agree, I'll do it."

He took the shot, but it didn't give him the numbness he wanted. It did nothing to dull the ache around his heart. He had a feeling after this was over, nothing ever would.

BECAUSE OF THE very public nature of Ari's disappearing act, Lydia Coogan was able to get an audience with the judge within twenty-four hours of her return. It was only through the fast-talking of Robert Barth that Pru and any of the family were present for the occasion to present their side. It wasn't enough time for Robert to work up any kind of a solid defense. They'd barely had time to fill him in on what was actually happening before making the collective pilgrimage to the courthouse, where they were nearly late for lack of parking.

"All rise for the Honorable Jefferson Moseley."

As she got to her feet, arm tight around Ari, Pru felt the first glimmer of hope. Judge Moseley had been on the bench since God was a boy. He himself had presided over her own adoption and that of all her sisters. He *knew* their family. That had to count for something.

But Judge Moseley wasn't looking friendly as he emerged from chambers and took the bench. His black hair had gone gray since Pru had last seen him. It stood out now in stark relief against his mahogany skin. His thick, salt and pepper brows drew down in a scowl over dark, serious eyes, and his mouth was a thin line of disapproval as he surveyed their group.

"Be seated."

Ari leaned over and whispered. "He's scary looking."

"Shhh," Pru murmured, giving her a squeeze.

Judge Moseley opened the file he'd carried in, presumably the complaint issued by Lydia Coogan. He read over it in silence before looking up at Pru and her sisters. "Well, this is certainly not what I'd expected to see you in my courtroom for."

Pru resisted the urge to duck her head in shame.

"I was sorry to hear about your mother."

"Thank you, sir."

He shifted his attention to the social worker, who sat at the opposite counsel's table on her own. "Miss Coogan, you're new to DHS in this region, are you not?"

"Yes, sir."

"You've taken on much of the caseload of Mae Bradley, while she's been out recovering from back surgery."

"That is correct, sir."

"Tell me why, exactly, you have dragged us all here today."

"As I explained in my report—"

"I'm not interested in reading your full report just now, Miss Coogan. I would like a succinct explanation why you are seeking an injunction to have the minor child, Ariana Rosas, removed from the care of Pru Reynolds and her fiancé Flynn Bohannon."

Annoyance rippled across the woman's features before she pulled herself together. "Quite simply, your honor, because they lied."

"About what, exactly?"

"The nature of their relationship. They did not meet two years ago, as indicated by Mr. Bohannon's exception to policy paperwork."

Judge Moseley looked back to their table. "Is this true?"

"Yes, your honor."

"If they lied on official paperwork, what else are they hiding? Add to that, the child ran away two days ago—"

"Because you were going to take me away!"

Ari shouted. "I heard you."

Judge Moseley looked at Ari and his expression softened a fraction. "You heard her?"

Ari hunched back against Pru. "I was eavesdropping. Sir. She said she was going to take me away from Pru and Flynn for no good reason."

"I *have* a reason," Lydia interrupted.

"Miss Coogan, it is not your turn to speak."

The woman sat back as if she'd been slapped.

"Ari, go ahead. Why did hearing that make you run?"

"Because I don't want to leave. I don't want to go anywhere with her. She's not like Mae. She's not nice, and she's more concerned with the rules than what's actually best for people. I was going to hide at Logan's until everything got straightened out."

"And who is Logan?" Judge Moseley asked.

"Logan Maxwell, your honor. A close family friend," Pru explained. "He has a farm about ten miles from our house."

"*Ten miles?* Holy crap, is it really that far?" Ari asked. "No wonder I didn't make it."

"I believe it's safe to say, your honor, that Ari wants to stay with Pru," Robert said.

"Duh," Ari answered.

Pru gave her hand a warning squeeze.

"The law is not about what people *want* but about what's right," Lydia said.

"Miss Coogan, you will not tell me in my own courtroom about what the law is or is not."

Flynn stood up. "Your honor, if I may have permission to speak? I'd like to address the allegations Miss Coogan has leveled against us."

"Granted." The judge leaned back in his seat and waited.

"I arrived in Eden's Ridge the last week of June, just a few days before Kennedy's wedding. That was the first time I met Pru. We were attracted to each other, and after the wedding, I opted to extend my stay to pursue that attraction."

Pru appreciated him leaving out the part where she'd propositioned him.

"When Miss Coogan became aware of the intimate nature of our relationship, I'm the one who lied in an effort to protect Pru. I'm not from here. I didn't know anything about how your foster system worked. But I wasn't willing for her involvement with me to in any way endanger her adoption of Ari. It was my lie. And I'm the one who convinced her and Ari and Kennedy, who I *have* known for years, to go along with it. I changed all my plans, and I stayed to make sure that everything happened as it should. And I fell in love with her. I fell in love with them both. I don't know at what point the lie became real, but it did."

Flynn turned to look at her, and Pru could swear there was apology in his eyes as he said, "I love this woman. It may not have been for as long as we claimed, but that doesn't make it any less real."

Pru smiled at him, so relieved to have him on her side, this whole ordeal seemed just a little less scary.

He turned back to the judge. "Don't judge

Pru's fitness as a parent based on her behavior since I came into her life. She is an amazing mother, and Ari shouldn't be anywhere else. I'm the problem in all of this. I'm the reason we're standing here. I'm the reason Miss Coogan wants to take Ari away." He paused, his throat working, before he squared his shoulders and looked at Judge Moseley. "So take me out of the equation. Let Ari stay with her mother, and I'll go."

There was a sound like a dying animal. A short, sharp cry of pain. Pru didn't realize it had come from her until everybody turned to look at her. But she could only stare at Flynn.

He was going to leave her. After everything they'd been through, he was going to leave. She'd be alone. Again. The shock of it was a stunning agony that left her breathless.

"No." The word came out barely above a whisper.

But Flynn heard it. He took a step toward her, his face twisted with regret. "*Mo chroí—*"

Ari exploded up from her seat. "Why are

adults so *stupid?*"

Horrified, Pru reached for her, but the girl jerked away.

"The rules are *stupid!*" Her shout echoed through the courtroom, all her teenage outrage spilling out in a torrent. "Flynn loves Pru. Period. End of story. Why should it matter when or for how long or why? The three of us are better together, and only a total *moron* would think otherwise."

It was all too much. Pru's world was positively crumbling around her. Flynn had just stabbed her through the heart, and her child was pitching a hissy fit in front of the man who would be deciding her fate. Somehow, she kept her voice even. "Honey, we don't call people stupid or morons."

She stamped her foot, flinging her arms out to encompass the entire assembly of adults in the room. "But they *are*, Mom!"

Robert cleared his throat in a way that sounded suspiciously like a laugh. "Uh, your honor, I beg the court's indulgence to present

some additional evidence as to the verisimili-
tude of the relationship between Miss Reynolds
and Mr. Bohannon."

"What evidence?" Lydia Coogan demanded.
She might have said more, but a sharp glance
from Judge Moseley shut her up.

"Counselor, approach the bench please."

Robert moved to the front of the courtroom
and spoke to the judge in a low voice. Pru kept
her eyes on him. She didn't dare look at Flynn
again. Not after that whole speech. She'd break,
and she didn't have that luxury.

"Very well, you may proceed."

With what? Pru wondered.

Robert strode to the back of the courtroom
and opened the doors. "Come on in."

People poured into the courtroom—Abbey,
Logan, Porter, Ford McIntosh, Crystal, Rev-
erend Hodgeson, Denver, Cayla, Clyde Parker,
Kacy and her parents. They kept on coming,
until it seemed half the population of Eden's
Ridge filled the rows of seats.

Pru leaned back to whisper to Kennedy,

"What are they all doing here?"

"I called them."

"Why?"

"Because I knew he was going to do this, and I wanted you both to have a fighting chance."

One after another, Robert called people up and asked them questions about Flynn, about their impressions of him, his involvement with the community since he came to Eden's Ridge, and about his relationship with Pru. One after another, they supported Pru and Flynn, as a couple and as prospective parents. With each testimony, Lydia Coogan's face flushed further.

When everyone was through, Robert faced the judge. "I believe evidence indicates the legitimacy of the relationship and the type of parents Miss Reynolds and Mr. Bohannon actually are."

Judge Moseley looked at Flynn. "Mr. Bohannon, you claim to love this woman."

"With all my heart, sir."

"Do you actually want to leave her?"

Flynn turned his gaze on Pru and she felt the punch of it down to her marrow. "No. I'd sooner have my fiddle hand broken."

"And do you actually want to walk away from this child?"

"Absolutely not, your honor."

The judge looked to the disgruntled social worker. "Your issue with this is?"

"They lied," she repeated, as if that outweighed everything else.

"About the length of their relationship. Were the intimacies of that relationship conducted in front of the child?"

"No! Of course not," Pru said.

"Then the child is endangered by this how, exactly?" Judge Moseley asked. "Because from where I'm sitting, I see a man who has turned his life upside down for love of them both. I hardly think that's a poor environment to raise a child in."

"What kind of a person gets engaged after a matter of days?" Lydia demanded. "How is that proof of a solid relationship?"

"I met and married my wife in a month, Miss Coogan," Judge Moseley said. "We just celebrated our fortieth anniversary. Sometimes, you just know."

The woman began to sputter. "But…the rules. They exist for a *reason*."

Judge Moseley looked at Ari and winked. "Sometimes the rules are stupid. Injunction denied."

The slamming of his gavel was the best sound Pru had ever heard.

Everybody in the courtroom cheered. Ari leapt up and threw her arms around Kennedy.

Flynn closed the distance between them and pulled her into a tight embrace. "I'm sorry. I'm so sorry I made you cry." He wiped away her tears. "But it's over. We won."

"You were going to leave." The truth of that, even now, had her wanting to crumble.

Regret streaked over his face. "It would have killed me. But I didn't see another choice." He stroked her cheek. "Forgive me?"

"Partners," she reminded him, taking a

fistful of his shirt and giving him a shake. "That was the deal we made. That means no more self-sacrificing decisions that don't include me."

"Never again," he promised.

As pressed his lips to hers, Pru felt her world shift back to its proper axis.

"Thankfully some of us were a little less extreme in our planning," Kennedy said, arm hooked around Ari's shoulders.

Head resting against Flynn's chest, Pru smiled at her sister. "Thank you."

Athena and Maggie clustered around them, each adding an arm to the family chain.

"I'd say a celebration is in order," Maggie said.

"What's an appropriate celebration for aversion of epic disaster combined with an engagement? Athena asked.

"I'd say Ari gets to pick," Xander added, coming to stand behind his wife.

"There is only one right answer to this question," Ari said, meeting Flynn's gaze. Grinning at each other, they shouted, "Pizza!"

EPILOGUE

"I'M SO GLAD YOU could make it!" Pru gave Mae a careful hug.

The older woman squeezed her hard. "I wouldn't have missed this for the world. I'm sorry my surgery and recovery kept me out of the loop for so long and brought you trouble."

They both looked across the room to where Ari and Flynn stood in animated conversation with his sister and brother-in-law beneath a hand-lettered banner that declared *Happy Gotcha Day, Ari!*

"It all worked out in the end. As of this afternoon, we're completely legit. Judge Moseley signed off on the adoption." She and Flynn were officially parents to a precocious fourteen-year-old girl, and life would never be the same again.

"That's wonderful! Your mother would be so pleased."

Pru felt an ache amid all the happy of having the adoption complete and the house full to the rafters with family. "I wish she could be here to see this. To know Flynn and how happy he makes me. And to see our family expand again. You know how much she loved that."

"I do. As much as I enjoyed helping her do it. I know she's looking down and smiling right now. She'd love seeing you and Kennedy settled."

"And be plotting some form of matchmaking to see that Maggie and Athena follow suit." Ari hadn't been the only hopeless romantic in the family.

"Any likely prospects on that front?" Mae asked with interest.

Pru glanced at Athena, who stood by the big Christmas tree with a glass of champagne, talking to Porter. "Not sure. Athena's been dating a guy from work back in Chicago for the past couple of months." Apparently whatever had passed between her and Logan at the wedding had been a one-time thing. If Logan was bothered by that, he hadn't let on. "And Maggie is…Maggie. A workaholic to the core."

"Their time will come," Mae said, with a knowing smile. "Love comes when you least expect it."

"Ain't it the truth," Pru agreed. "You know, it helps, having you here. It makes me miss Mom a little bit less."

"She'd be so proud of what you've done here with the inn. And what is it going on next door?"

"Our day spa is finally finished. We did a soft launch and an open house last week so we can start selling gift certificates in time for the holidays, but we don't have the grand opening until after the new year." Pru looped an arm through Mae's. "You should schedule an appointment. We'll give you the family discount."

Mae beamed. "I will absolutely do that! Now, why don't you introduce me to your Flynn?"

"Gladly." Pru escorted her through the crowd of people who'd shown up for the adoption party. "Flynn, I want you to meet Mae Bradley, a dear family friend. Mae, my fiancé, Flynn Bohannon."

Flynn grinned and took Mae's hand. "Miss Bradley, I've heard many good things. You're recovering well from surgery?"

"Slowly but surely, thank you. Congratulations on your new family."

He hooked an arm around Ari's shoulders. "I have the best daughter in the world, and that's the truth of it."

Ari snuggled in, a matching grin on her face. "We'll pretend he isn't biased."

"I'm not biased. My entire family agrees, don't you?"

The Bohannons—all six of them, who'd come over from Ireland for the adoption—shouted agreement.

"There, you see?"

His mother Moira laughed. "He's a proud da."

"And a good one," Ari declared.

"The best," Pru murmured, her eyes going misty.

"Here now, there'll be no tears today, *mo mhuirnín.*" Flynn tipped her face up for a kiss.

"Happy tears," Pru promised. "I've been a little watery all day."

"A woman's entitled to cry a few happy tears on the day she gains a daughter." Moira punctuated the pronouncement with a lift of her glass.

"Oh, I don't have anything to toast with."

She tucked an arm through Pru's. "Then let's rectify that, shall we?" Before Pru could object, she was being steered toward the kitchen.

"Once they were away from the others,

Moira plucked some tissues from a box and handed them over. "There now. I thought you could use a minute."

Pru sniffed and dabbed at her eyes. "Thanks. I'm so happy today. It's just, I'm missing my mother."

"Sure, and it's no wonder. I know you wish she were here."

"So much. I wish she could've known Flynn. He's such a very good man, and I'm so lucky he came into my life."

Moira skimmed a hand over Pru's hair in a gesture so redolent of Joan, it made her throat ache. "I didn't know your mother, but I've gotten to know you these past months. It takes a fine woman to raise someone as wonderful as you. We're delighted you'll be part of our family."

"Oh, Moira." Pru felt the waterworks starting up again. "Thank you. I can only hope that I do half as good a job with Ari."

"You and Flynn have taken to parenthood beautifully, you have. Ari's a darlin' girl."

"She makes it easy. She's a great kid."

"She absolutely is. We're all besotted with her." She plucked a glass off a tray on the counter and handed it to Pru. "Now that the adoption is finalized, the two of you should be looking toward picking a wedding date. That should be sooner rather than later, I'm thinkin'." Moira's eyes, so like Flynn's, twinkled.

Pru blinked at her, then looked down at the glass of sparkling cider she'd picked up instead of champagne. "I…oh my God."

"Leaked like a sieve with both of mine," she said cheerfully.

Pru felt faint. "I need to talk to Flynn."

Her future mother-in-law grinned and wrapped her in a hug. "Topping off a day of joy with more joy is always a good idea."

In something of a daze, Pru wandered back into the party. She must have looked as shell-shocked as she felt, because he immediately broke away and crossed to her.

"What is it?"

"I need some air." She laced her fingers

with his. Kennedy caught her eye from across the room and started forward, but Pru just shook her head. With their family, this wasn't a secret that would stay secret long. But Flynn needed to be the first to know.

They stepped out into the early winter dark. The chill made her skin pebble, but she relished the good, clean air. It didn't seem like her lungs were working quite right. She pulled Flynn around the corner, then just turned and burrowed into his arms. They came around her in an instant.

"What's wrong, *agra*?"

"Nothing's wrong. I'm happy. I'm so damned happy, Flynn." She lifted her face and knew she was starting to cry again.

He brushed at the tears and offered a sympathetic smile. "Sure, and there's plenty of reason for it. We gained a daughter today."

Pru sucked in a breath and stepped back, laying a hand on her belly. "We gained more than that."

Flynn just stared at her. "I don't understand."

"You're a father twice over."

"I'm—" His mouth dropped open and he covered her hand with his. "Truly?"

"I haven't taken a test yet, but I think so."

Flynn scooped her off her feet with a whoop. "This is wonderful!"

"Really? You're not upset?"

"Upset? Why would I be upset?"

"Well, we weren't exactly planning on this."

"*Mo stór,* we haven't exactly planned on anything, and life with you has been the best possible surprise. I love you."

The kiss he laid on her left no doubt of that.

"We have to tell Ari," he said.

"Not yet. Let's wait. I don't want her to feel like her day is overshadowed."

"Are you kidding? This is *awesome!*"

With a laugh, Pru dropped her head to Flynn's chest as Ari bounced out from around the corner of the house. "You're never going to stop eavesdropping, are you?"

"Probably not. Then I'd miss all the good stuff. I'm really gonna have a sister or brother?"

"Looks that way. It seems the Reynolds-Bohannon family is going to be expanding faster than we'd expected." Pru rocked back on her heels as Ari threw her arms around them both.

"Best. Day. Ever."

As she stood in a tangle of arms with the man she loved and the child of her heart, Pru couldn't help but agree.

~

Choose Your Next Romance

GUESS WHAT? That whole wedding fling between Athena and Logan? Not the end of them. In *Stay A Little Longer,* Book 3 of The Misfit Inn series, you finally find out what drives our favorite prickly chef and get a view inside to her marshmallow center. Loaded with plenty of family and lots of matchmaking Ari, you won't want to miss it!

You can also see some more of the Reynolds-Bohannon family in my connected Rescue My Heart series, starting with *Baby It's Cold Outside*. This one is a snowbound, forced-cohabitation romance between a former Army Ranger and a runaway writer. There's hilarity and heat and a really fun Ari cameo

OTHER BOOKS BY KAIT NOLAN

A complete and up-to-date list of all my books can be found at https://kaitnolan.com.

THE MISFIT INN SERIES
SMALL TOWN FAMILY ROMANCE

- *When You Got A Good Thing* (Kennedy and Xander)
- *Til There Was You* (Misty and Denver)

- *Those Sweet Words* (Pru and Flynn)
- *Stay A Little Longer* (Athena and Logan)
- *Bring It On Home* (Maggie and Porter)

RESCUE MY HEART SERIES
SMALL TOWN MILITARY ROMANCE

- *Baby It's Cold Outside* (Ivy and Harrison)
- *What I Like About You* (Laurel and Sebastian)
- *Bad Case of Loving You* (Paisley and Ty prequel)
- *Made For Loving You* (Paisley and Ty)

MEN OF THE MISFIT INN
SMALL TOWN SOUTHERN ROMANCE

- *Let It Be Me* (Emerson and Caleb)
- *Our Kind of Love* (Abbey and Kyle)

WISHFUL SERIES

SMALL TOWN SOUTHERN ROMANCE

- *Once Upon A Coffee* (Avery and Dillon)
- *To Get Me To You* (Cam and Norah)
- *Know Me Well* (Liam and Riley)
- *Be Careful, It's My Heart* (Brody and Tyler)
- *Just For This Moment* (Myles and Piper)
- *Wish I Might* (Reed and Cecily)
- *Turn My World Around* (Tucker and Corinne)
- *Dance Me A Dream* (Jace and Tara)
- *See You Again* (Trey and Sandy)
- *The Christmas Fountain* (Chad and Mary Alice)
- *You Were Meant For Me* (Mitch and Tess)
- *A Lot Like Christmas* (Ryan and Hannah)
- *Dancing Away With My Heart* (Zach and Lexi)

WISHING FOR A HERO SERIES (A WISHFUL SPINOFF SERIES)
SMALL TOWN ROMANTIC SUSPENSE

- *Make You Feel My Love* (Judd and Autumn)
- *Watch Over Me* (Nash and Rowan)
- *Can't Take My Eyes Off You* (Ethan and Miranda)
- *Burn For You* (Sean and Delaney)

MEET CUTE ROMANCE
SMALL TOWN SHORT ROMANCE

- *Once Upon A Snow Day*
- *Once Upon A New Year's Eve*
- *Once Upon An Heirloom*
- *Once Upon A Coffee*
- *Once Upon A Campfire*
- *Once Upon A Rescue*

SUMMER CAMP
CONTEMPORARY ROMANCE

- *Once Upon A Campfire*
- *Second Chance Summer*

ACKNOWLEDGMENTS

More than any I've written in a long while, this book would not have been possible without the *detailed* feedback from a number of people who know more about stuff than I do!

Enormous thanks to Angela Van Cleave Albers for allowing me to endlessly pick her brain about the legalities of the foster system and all things adoption. She basically is Joan Reynolds, and there's a special place in heaven waiting just for her someday.

To Taylor Holden for making sure Flynn sounds appropriately Irish. *Go raibh maith agat.*

To Bryan Handzus for his patient responses to my probably insane questions about search and rescue (and his mama, Stacey, for introducing us!).

As always, my undying devotion to my editor, Susan Bischoff, for holding my hand when I thought I couldn't do this.

And to the Squee Squad, for your enthusiastic support of my work. Y'all are why I do what I do.

ABOUT KAIT

Kait is a Mississippi native, who often swears like a sailor, calls everyone sugar, honey, or darlin', and can wield a bless your heart like a saber or a Snuggie, depending on requirements.

You can find more information on this

RITA ® Award-winning author and her books on her website http://kaitnolan.com. While you're there, sign up for her newsletter so you don't miss out on news about new releases!